FALLING FOR HIS STEP-SISTER

ALIE GARNETT

For my Family for all their support.

THE LOVELY'S

Sera Lovely –35-year-old who is the Director of HR, mom of 7, engaged to Harrison Dean (the longest engagement in the history of the world.)

Harper Lovely Hawthorne - 30-year-old who is owner of Lovely Catering, with Lucy's help, the new wife of Kaine Hawthorne and they are helping each other to relax and focus on something other than work.

Mabel Lovely Scott - 28-year-old who is a Twin to Lucy, Children's Lit professor, married to Clifton Scott V. Working on being a better sister to everyone.

Lucy Lovely - 28-year-old who is a Twin to Mabel, Works for Lovely catering and cleans offices. Best friend to Cliff Scott.

Agatha Lovely - 26-year-old who is an amazing artist and mediocre bartender looking for a job.

Beatrix Potter (Buzz) Lovely – 25-year-old reporter for the times, youngest and more outgoing of the big girls. (Psst: if you have a lead on a good story, Buzz needs a break)

CHAPTER ONE

JONAS RAIDEN'S step-monster Judith Rowley was the reason he was never getting married. Ever. She was rude and opinionated and could argue until she was blue in the face—it didn't matter if she was right or wrong. She was going to argue the point into the ground. Most of the time, she was wrong.

Twenty years ago, his dad had married her in a lavish, over-the-top ceremony that Jonas had been forced to take part in. Since that day, she had not grown on Jonas; she was more like a fungus that you tried to get rid of, but it just kept showing up a few weeks later, no matter what you tried. It got more annoying each time it happened until you just lived with it in disgust.

Jonas wasn't the only one who thought that. His dad had left her three years ago—and not for the first time. This time, however, he had moved to a completely new town to get away from her, leaving behind almost everything as he did. His only mistake in the move had been to not divorce the woman, a simple step that would have prevented her from being there tonight. Yet here she was, sitting across from him, prattling on about some staff member who had walked out that morning. This was the third staff member to leave since she had walked into the house just a few months before.

His dad, George Raiden, was staring at his plate as if it had the answers to the universe on it instead of salmon. The only answer that Jonas wanted was why his stepmother was here, and why wasn't he told before he showed up for supper. Except Jonas knew the answer to that question, and she was sitting next to her mother in rapt attention. Louisa was the spitting image of her mother in looks and, sadly, personality.

Louisa was his younger half-sister, and at nineteen, he barely knew her. Since he had avoided her mother for years, he had avoided her as well, which he saw now as a mistake. He had missed a lot of her life; she was an adult now. When had that happened?

Dr. Judith Rowley, because she was too important to take her husband's name, turned to him and drew him back into the conversation. "It's nice that you can make time to eat with us, Jonas. I haven't seen you once since Louisa and I came home. Isn't that right, George?" She shot her husband a look that said she didn't want her stepson there now either.

His father looked up from his plate and over at his wife. He hadn't been listening and was now caught not knowing that was happening. Two slow blinks later, he dismissed the entire group and went back to looking at his plate.

Saving his father from answering, he told her, "I have been busy at work. Being the VP at Raiden & Son's Financial takes a lot of my time."

It was vague enough that she would be satisfied, but not enough that she would ask anymore. There was no way he was ever telling her the truth about his job ... or anything else about his life. He had learned long ago that if he kept his answers light, she would stop talking about it. After all, she wasn't interested if she wasn't talking about herself.

For years, he had worked with his uncle at the family company, a company his dad had opted out of to stay in academia. Jonas thought that he would one day work his way to the top of the company, taking over from his uncle and mentor. That was now in the balance.

"You're still there, then? I had thought you would find something better." Judith's brown eyes were full of judgment.

"We can't all be academics."

His stepmother didn't think you had achieved anything until you had a master's degree, and a doctorate almost made her swoon. But Jonas had never been so happy to graduate with a degree and walk away from academia. He had never looked back.

When Jonas had first met his stepmom, he was fourteen and hated her the moment they had met. For months, he had called her Dr. Judith, even as she had moved into George's house. The name had never bothered her, and he just grew tired of it, so he spent the rest of his teen years ignoring her.

Since the beginning, his dad had let her have her way with everything. By the time she had moved her boxes in, she was pressuring his dad to marry her. The pressure had worked, and within months, they were married. By then, she was obviously pregnant, and George was ecstatic about having another child.

The marriage had been far from happy from Jonas's point of view. In nineteen years, they had separated no less than seven times, and typically, it would last for nearly a year. But then something would happen, and they would be back together again. There was just something about the woman that kept his dad going back ... or letting her come back.

"You just didn't have the ambition," Judith told him with a dismissive wave.

Jonas bit his tongue to stop himself from telling her that he didn't think *she* had ambition. After all these years, he still didn't know much about her life before she moved in with his dad. Just that she had been a professor when they had met at a conference for children's literature, which was what they both taught. She had promptly quit to raise Louisa.

At the time, George was already a department head in Chicago, and Judith was from some other college somewhere. Exactly where was still unknown to Jonas. In order for her to move in with George, she had to quit her job. So far, she hadn't looked for another one that he was aware of.

"Well, you must come home more often since we are all in the same town now. We missed you for the holidays; you must have been out of town." Judith wasn't all that convincing, which was fine. He almost laughed at her words about him missing the holidays, which was just the week before. He hadn't been invited, and he didn't want to be.

He hadn't celebrated a holiday with his family since he'd graduated high school and had chosen a college in a city that was far away from his parents. Not being close to his stepmom had been enough reason to not see his father and his sister for years. After college, he had gone to work for the company his grandfather had built, which was still not in the same town as his parents, who had lived in Chicago almost all his life. Until now.

Yet now here he was once again, eating with her, trapped in a conversation that he didn't want to be in. His dad and sister were silent as church mice.

"Yeah, it's too bad I was busy," he told her, then turned to his sister. "How are classes, Louisa?"

His sister had just completed her first semester in college and was going to start a new one the next week. Jonas remembered that time as exciting and fun. But he had been away from Judith, not under the same roof like his sister.

"It's going wonderfully, and she's excelling in her classes," her mother answered for her. To her credit, Louisa had opened her mouth, but she hadn't been fast enough to actually answer.

At nineteen, he was surprised the girl let her mother speak for her. Most teenagers resented their parents, but not Louisa. All she did was slowly blink her blue eyes a few times like George always did.

"Are you excited for any particular one this semester?" he asked with interest, hoping she would get to answer. He hadn't spent much time with her as an adult. Being attached to her mother's hip made that impossible.

"The one on Dickens." Judith patted her on the back, but Louisa turned away and took a bite of the fish, completely giving up and letting her mother do the talking for her.

"Dickens is good but may be depressing for an entire semester. If it were me, I would be watching all the movies I could find on the subject. Less reading that way," he told his stepmother as he watched his sister suppress a smile. Judith couldn't quite figure out if he was kidding or not—which he wasn't. But Louisa's smile caused him to see her as more than just Judith's puppet. She just didn't feel a conversation with him was worth the fight with her mom, which hurt.

"You just don't understand the classics, Jonas. I don't expect you to be well-read, even if I know who your father is." Judith looked over at George. His father was known far and wide for his expertise in classic literature. Adult or children's, it didn't matter. George knew it.

"I'm as well-read as the next guy, just maybe not the classics. But then again, isn't your doctorate in children's literature? Isn't that what you taught when you bothered to teach? Of course, that was so long ago, I wouldn't expect you to remember." Jonas was hoping to rile her up because once she stomped away, he could just talk to his dad like he wanted, and possibly Louisa.

Unfortunately, it didn't work. Her nose flared in anger, and then she decided to ignore him by going back to her conversation about the chef walking out on her and how she had to order in their meal. She now had to hire someone to take the chef's place. Jonas had never seen her cook anything more elaborate than boxed cereal.

An hour later, he was the one who couldn't take anymore. He had spent the entire evening only conversing with Judith. His dad hadn't said a word, and Judith didn't let Louisa say more than one or two words at a time.

Getting up from the table, he was silent as he headed for the door. He was done.

On the drive to the Beckman Hotel, he wondered how long his dad would last this time. The moment he had retired, he had walked away from his wife. Now she was here, and he already looked ready to bolt. Not that he blamed the man, except Jonas would have divorced her years ago—many, many years ago.

He wished that he could just go back to his house and forget about the entire hotel thing, except his friend and lawyer had told him to rent a hotel room for the duration of the investigation. It hadn't even started yet, and he was ready for it to be over with so that he could get on with his life. Except, what was his life going to be like when it was over? He was blowing the whistle on his uncle, who was Jonas's soon-to-be-former boss. And he was sure that the family connection wouldn't mean much after the dust was settled.

For a moment, Jonas debated on whether or not he should call his lawyer to see if there was anything else he should know. Yesterday he had talked to federal agents the entire day; today, he had spent another half of the day with them. Now it was just a waiting game for when the building was raided. Each day he was pretending to be sick until the shit hit the fan.

Except it was late, and his lawyer was getting married in a few days and was probably busy enjoying his last days of freedom. Also, Harrison Dean would contact him if something actually came up.

When he had noticed that there were discrepancies in the accounts at Raiden & Son's Financial, he had called the cops, who had told him to hire a lawyer. The first name that had come to mind had been his fraternity brother, who was working at one of the top law firms in the country.

At one time, he and Harrison had been close, close enough that he had been in the man's first wedding. Jonas had also gotten an invitation to Harrison's second wedding, which might have been what had spurned him to contact the man. Jonas needed a friend, not just a lawyer.

Walking into his hotel room, he sensed that something was off. It was just a feeling that made the hair on the back of his neck raise. Looking around the living room area, he saw nothing.

When he had contacted the feds about his uncle, he hadn't thought anything of it. The more they dug, however, the more it seemed his uncle had a lot to lose by getting caught. It had been them who had suggested that there was a possibility of danger, something he hadn't felt until right then.

Pulling out his cell phone, he started to dial the hotel to get security when he caught a glimpse of someone in his closet. A flash of long, bright red hair made him set his phone down, the number only half-entered.

He had no idea who it was or why she was there, but he was sure she wasn't a threat to him. Either way, he wanted to get her out of the room just the same. But for a moment, his mind was off his troubles and on her. Seeing how far she was willing to go for whatever brought her here.

Slowly, he started to disrobe as he walked across the room to see how fast she would run. After an evening with his stepmother, he needed to have fun for a few minutes.

CHAPTER TWO

WATCHING the sexiest man she had ever seen stripping right in front of her made one thing clear: this was definitely going to get her in deep trouble. In fact, she was probably going to be grounded for life, but it was going to be so worth it. Her mom might even applaud her for her initiative and creativity—or she was going to kick her out of the family.

Whichever happens, Beatrix Lovely had no way out of the situation now. She was already in the closet, and there was no coming out of it now. Well, she could hide in it all night, but then she would be fired, and her career as a reporter would be over.

Tonight, she was getting the scoop on her mom's fiancé's newest client. Harrison had let it slip that his college buddy, Jonas Raiden, was going to blow the whistle on his boss for embezzling from their company. Buzz had spent two days researching Raiden & Son's Financial and everyone involved, and now she was going to pounce on the man for an interview—an interview that was going to make her a household name.

Well, not her actual name, but her pen name: Bea Bradford. Bea Lovely just wasn't going to cut it with hard-hitting news like this.

Jonas had been staying at the hotel for days in order to stay away from his uncle and anyone his uncle knew. Once federal agents raid the company, the reporters would be there. Instead of waiting for that to happen, she was going to be first in line. Bea Bradford was going to get the scoop. She would be famous.

Sure, she knew she shouldn't ambush him in his hotel room, but Sera had told her that Harrison had said, "no questions and no snooping," so under no circumstances was she going to get an interview with the man. What Harrison didn't know was that when Mom says no, you sneak around her back. It had been that way forever.

Harrison might not know the rule, but he should have suspected it. After all, he had been dating the woman for a few months and was marrying her. By now, he had to know that her daughters didn't exactly listen to her. It wasn't something they actually hid from him, or from her for that matter.

Not that Sera Lovely was Buzz's real mom; she was her stepmom. Her real mom had skipped out on her five girls years before Sera had shown up in their lives, and now when any of them said, "mom," they were talking about Sera.

It was just a coincidence that Sera was marrying Jonas's lawyer and that they'd had a private whispered conversation about what was happening where Buzz could hear them. That was pure luck on Buzz's part, and Buzz was going to get the scoop on him before everything happened because she was the best reporter for the best paper in town. However, she was going to be fired if she didn't come through with the article. She had to get this interview.

Since she never got any good assignment, she had lied to her editor and said she already knew the man and that she knew that there was something brewing. Not that she shared what it was, just that it was going to be big. Besides that, she should already know the man since he was her near-stepdad's best friend or something. She should've been able to get an interview and not be barred by Sera's no questions rule. *Maddening*.

It had been by luck that she had gotten into the room when the maid was there five hours before. So, for the last five hours, she had been hiding in the closet, waiting. Minutes before Jonas had walked in, she had been bored because her phone had only twenty percent of its battery left, and she needed that to record her interview—an interview she was in no way not getting now. The rest of her phone's battery had been wasted on addictive games to keep her mind off her mom's impending anger and her own boredom.

The sun had set hours ago when her phone had buzzed in her hand, and she answered it, bored as hell in the closet. And at that point, she was about to give up on the man ever coming back.

"Buzz," she barked at her oldest sister. If it had been anyone else, she would've answered nicely with, "Bea Bradford," but her sister didn't deserve nice.

"Where the fuck are you? You were supposed to be here an hour ago!" Harper yelled at her.

Rolling her eyes, she remembered that she had promised her sister she would help her out today. Harper and Lucy owned a catering company, and Buzz usually helped out in the evenings when she could. Today she had to put her career in front of her sisters'. Recently, Lucy had started a new job as a personal assistant and had less time for catering than before, which was leaving Harper short-staffed a lot more than usual.

Not remembering where "here" was and not caring, she answered, "Working. I have a job, you know."

"Barely, Buzz. You should be more focused on helping me," the oldest Lovely sister complained as she always did.

"You're saying I need to focus on waitressing?" Buzz questioned. She usually helped her sister two to three times a week at best. Was that what she should be focusing on? Buzz could tell Lucy wasn't there and that Harper was a little stressed, something that Harper rarely showed.

"Or something that pays and doesn't take all your time, and something you are good at."

"I can't help you tonight. Another time," she said. Being a waitress for a catering company wasn't what she wanted to do with her life, especially one that was run by Harper.

"You better remember that I need you tomorrow night. No

pretending to work." Harper hung up on her, and Buzz scowled at her phone. No way was she helping her with her event tomorrow.

Turning her phone off, she closed her eyes in the dark closet. Yes, she'd work for Harper tomorrow; her sister needed her, so she'd go. Harper was doing fantastic with her catering business, and even if her fiancé was requesting that she cut back, she was still busy and needed her other sisters even more. At least there were three other sisters to help her out.

The closet was hot, or maybe just a woman sitting in the closet for five hours had made the closet hot. A few hours ago, she had unbuttoned the white blouse she wore, happy she had worn a tank top this morning. Both of which might not be salvageable after a night in a steam closet. Good thing both had been borrowed from her sister, so she didn't have to care that they were ruined.

Resting her eyes, she blew a wayward strand of red hair from her face as she tried to ignore the sweat running down her back. It was a good thing that it wasn't a video interview because she was sure she looked like garbage.

Not for the first time did she think she was making a mistake; maybe just getting his number and giving him a call would have worked. She should have ignored Sera and just asked, especially if Harrison put in a good word for her, which he would. She was, after all, his favorite almost stepdaughter. She was sure of it.

She tapped the bifold doors open a tiny bit with her foot to get some air in the little closet. She could swear she could feel the cool tufts of air teasing her. This had been a big mistake. Huge.

Just then, the door to the hotel suite opened and closed. Buzz heard jingling change and footsteps on the carpet—nothing to indicate the man wasn't alone. What would she do if he has company? That had never crossed her mind.

It seemed like he was in the living room area of the suite for a lifetime, and Buzz had no idea what he was doing. But it was probably time to get out of the closet and get her interview. Either get it done or get kicked out. With any luck, she wouldn't get arrested.

Except she froze when he came into view. He had already taken off his gray shirt. Buzz had seen a few pictures of Jonas, but in person, the man was worth remembering. Tall and lean, his dark hair and dark eyes were simply gorgeous. Jonas was mouth-wateringly handsome.

Buzz couldn't stop staring at the man through the crack in the door. The pictures didn't do him justice at all—they had never shown the muscles on his chest and arms. *How much did this man work out, every day?* she thought to herself. If she hadn't been hot before he came in, she was certainly hot now ... in a completely different way.

As she watched, he shed the black pants and laid them on the dresser, leaving him in tight white boxer shorts that left nothing to the imagination, *nothing*. Which just meant that she was in the closet for the night or forever, because she was not doing an interview with a nearly naked man. Nor was she going to announce her presence to one. It was starting to dawn on her that she had messed this up completely.

Jonas Raiden sat on the end of the bed, right in her perfect line of vision through the crack in the closet, and pulled off his socks, casually tossing them one after another on the floor. Both landed very close to the closet, too close for Buzz's comfort. That was why she was shifting in her seat, not any other reason.

Before she knew what he was going to do next, he stood with a cocky grin and slowly slid off the white boxers to reveal his not-so-hidden before penis. A very nice one, in Buzz's opinion. Silently slamming her hand over her mouth, she suppressed a groan at the sight. If he were dating someone, they were lucky—very lucky indeed.

Sitting back down, he was still facing her as he took his penis in his hand and stroked it a few times, leaning back a little as he did it. His eyes were on the closet she was in. It was well worth the wait for this. It wasn't going to make it onto paper, but it would make a good memory for lonely nights. Lonely, jobless nights.

"Come out and help me," he said, looking right at the closet she was in.

Sitting stock-still, she hoped that he had brought someone else home with him. Anyone else. Someone who was still in the living room area of the suite, despite him being naked in the bedroom. *Please don't let him have seen me in the closet,* she prayed.

Another firm stroke. "You, red, in the closet. Come out."

"No, thank you." Her voice sounded shaky even to her. Her eyes were still on him, but her mind was looking for a way out of this.

"This is what you came for, isn't it?" He held the erection in his hand. Suddenly, she wished she had just walked out of the closet hours ago.

"Fuck," she hissed under her breath. Her only option was to barrel out and hope he didn't recognize her at the wedding if he went. Maybe she shouldn't go to the wedding just in case. Maybe she should just leave the country altogether—her mom was definitely going to kill her for this. Her entirely awesome plan had completely backfired.

"Maybe that too." Her heart rate picked up as she watched him stand and walk towards the doors. He casually slid them open.

"Hello," she said weakly.

"Hello." He held out his hand to her as he looked her over, appraising her from head to toe. Buzz knew what she looked like after hours in the hot closet, and it wasn't good. Her hair was probably curled and damp, and her clothes were sticking to her right down to her black skirt.

Buzz grabbed his hand because she had nowhere else to go, and he pulled her to her feet. With her hand encased in his, he brought her towards the bed until he had sat down. Once seated, he pulled her close to him and slid his hands over her body. Buzz stood stock-still, frozen with fear. Though fear might not have been the feeling that was rushing through her body, that was something else.

He easily unbuttoned her skirt with a flick of his finger. "Name?"

"T-Trixi," she said lamely. Yes, it sounded just like it felt: hookerish.

The name brought a sexy smirk to his lips, a smirk she shouldn't like but did. Way too much. He knew she was lying and didn't seem to care.

"Well, Trixi, how much do you charge? Or are you here for something else?" He slid the skirt down her hips. For some reason, she couldn't stop him, didn't even want to.

This was her chance to get the interview. She was now in her panties, but it was an interview just the same—a good one.

Or maybe this wasn't the time to bring up the paper, to tell this man that was naked in front of her that she worked for the biggest paper in town. A paper he could easily sue because of that.

"I, uh … got lost," she stammered as his strong, warm hands pulled down her panties as easily as the skirt. His dark eyes never left hers, not looking down at what his hands were revealing.

"In my closet?" His eyebrow went up in question, but his hands slid her button-up shirt off her shoulders, then let it flutter softly to the floor to join her skirt and panties.

Thoughts of running away from this man were long gone. What little interaction they were having shouldn't have been enough to keep her there, wanting his touch, but it was. All she wanted, all she longed for was his next touch.

"This isn't my room?" she threw out as a possible reason for her being in that location.

The answer made him laugh, causing her knees to go weak. Or maybe it was his hands that were doing that, because the tank top was gone, and her breasts were now free of the bra that had been holding them not a second before. He was quick, but not quick enough for her.

"Do you want to be here, Trixi?" His eyes swept over her body in question.

He hadn't touched her skin yet, the feather-light brushes as he removed her clothes notwithstanding, but every fiber in her wanted him everywhere, touching everything. It was driving her to distraction that he didn't touch her.

"I, uhm … I …" She should've said, "no," but the word wouldn't come out. Such an easy word to say until his eyes swept her body again, and his tongue slipped out to wet his lips, all of which she wanted desperately on her body. Her resolve completely flew out the window, and her words sounded foreign as she whimpered, "yes."

Instantly, he wrapped his hands around her hips and pulled her closer to him. His hot breath brushed her nipple, causing her entire body to tremble slightly. His tongue snaked out and slipped across her beaded flesh, causing her involuntary moan of, "yes."

Deftly, he rolled her onto the bed under him. It happened so fast that Buzz lost her breath as his mouth fully captured her breast and suckled hard, making her gasp at the sensation. She didn't think she had ever been this turned on in her life.

"Holy fuck," she moaned as he did the same to the other one.

"You like that, Trixi?" he demanded and then gently bit down on her pebbled nipple, making her gasp.

As he bit down, his fingers slid lightly over her wet folds, and she jerked at the sensations it caused. Closing her eyes, she banished any remaining thoughts of leaving as she let her entire body focus on the feeling this guy was sending through her.

"Open your eyes, red. Don't want you to miss anything," his voice said into her ear, making her shiver with both fright and anticipation. Opening her eyes at his request, she met his intense gaze as his finger slid into her, making her shudder. But she held her eyes open as those fingers began to move rhythmically, in and out.

It was as if they had been doing this together forever; he played her body perfectly. From his lips on her breasts to his fingers finding a seductive rhythm, he knew the prefect beat. It had never been like this with someone for Buzz, not even close.

He grinned at her when she drew up her legs so that he had better access, and waves of pleasure coursed through her body as his fingers started to increase their speed. His thumb brushed her clit at the exact moment she needed it. Throwing her head back, her eyes closed as she chanted his name in the semi-dark room.

She laid on the bed, her body useless. He rolled her onto her stomach, and she went. She had just had the best orgasm of her life and couldn't move. Pulling the pillow under her head, she sighed and closed her eyes. Fuck, that had felt good. Now she just wanted to sleep and get out of there.

His hand swept down her back like he was petting a kitten. Long solid strokes: one, two, then he slapped her ass, hard.

"Hey!" Her head snapped up, and she turned to glare at him. That was uncalled for.

His only response was to bite her on the ass cheek. Taking her hips in his hands, he lifted them until her head fell back on the pillow. With her ass in the air and his hands on her hips, he slid into her in one smooth motion.

All her mind could think was, *How had it taken so long for him to get there?* This is what she had been waiting forever for—if forever was as long as he had been in the room with her, which felt like an eternity.

"Condom. Condom. Please say you have one," were the only words she could force from her mouth as he slid almost the entire way out of her and then back in quickly.

"Taken care of, Trixi." He slapped her ass again as he increased speed, and his other hand gripped her hips.

Matching his thrusts, she moaned at each one until his muscled arms lifted her body off the bed, and he continued to plow into her. At the new angle, she knew she was going to come, hard and fast. Unable to stop herself, she let it roll through her. She would have dropped to the bed in exhaustion, but he still held her and was still sliding in and out but at a more leisurely pace.

After lowering her to the bed, she sighed as he slid out of her. She could sleep for weeks now. It had been a while since she'd had good sex, and never had she had sex *this* good before.

Buzz was half-sad it was over, but her body was spent. With her eyes closed, she pulled the pillow back under her head. His hand slid down her back again, and she let out a low, appreciative moan.

In a heartbeat, she was looking at the ceiling, and he was sliding back into her. He gathered her hands in his and held them over her head as he looked into her eyes.

"Not done yet, Trixi." He said the name very slowly with an added emphasis on the ending, and she knew he was saying her name all the time because he knew it was fake. But it really could have been if he had wanted it to be that.

Wrapping her legs around him, she had thought that her body was done with him, but he had that magic touch, and it was humming back to life. At that point, she was so sensitive that every thrust sent shivers through her body.

Her orgasm came within moments, and as she writhed and moaned, she felt him stiffen and groan on top of her. Once he was done, he collapsed on top of her, and she didn't care at all. As she lay there, she caressed his muscled arms and back, then ran her fingers through his hair.

When she had fallen asleep, she hadn't known, but when she opened her eyes later, the clock beside the bed read 3 a.m. Buzz was more than willing to stay in that hotel room forever, but when her mind cleared, she came to her senses a little bit. Gently, she pushed him away from her, and he rolled away willingly in sleep. Sitting up, she looked over at his sleeping form in the bright lights of the room.

He was still gloriously naked, and all those amazing muscles were on display since they had not even pulled back the comforter. In sleep, he didn't make her lose her ever-loving mind, which meant she could think. And what she was thinking was that in a short amount of time, he was going to be at Sera and Harrison's wedding, and she would be unable to hide from him. At that point, he would know exactly who "Trixi" was, and everyone would know what she had done to ruin her career.

Slipping on her clothes quietly, she hoped that he would not remember her by then. He must have sex with dozens of women a month, possibly a week—no way was he going to remember her. Maybe she should do something about her hair; hair changes a woman.

Grabbing her phone from the closet, she knew she was going to be grounded for this. No way was she getting away with fucking Harrison's biggist client. She never got away with anything.

CHAPTER THREE

THE INSTANT HE WOKE UP, Jonas knew he was alone—naked and alone. Not that he didn't expect it, but it was disappointing just the same. More disappointing was that he had no idea who she was, but she sure as hell wasn't Trixi. And as far as he could tell, she was no longer in his closet. It was the first place his eyes went when she wasn't in the bed.

Rolling over, he still wanted her back in bed and naked, no matter her name. Finding her in his closet had been straight from a dream. She'd been a hot mess of a redhead with a smug grin and no fear.

His plan to scare her out of the closet had been thrown out the window the moment he had seen her. Once she had walked out of the closet, he was no longer interested in scaring her away. He had wanted to have sex with her instantly.

The woman was exactly his type, from her cocky little grin to her hot mess of a self with red hair. Her body had fit right into his hands, and she'd turned to putty as soon as he'd touched her.

It had pained him to ask if she'd wanted him, knowing that if she'd said no, he would've had let her go. Sure, it would have been painful to see her sashay from his life, but he would've let it happen. That she had wanted it just as bad had turned him on even more. Watching her orgasm once had been amazing, so much so that he'd made her come over and over again just so he could watch her scream. Even the memory of it made him want her back in his bed.

He had no idea why she had been in his closet. His only conclusion was that she was in the wrong room, and it had turned out well for him—and he hoped it was great for her also.

Sitting up in bed, he looked at the snow-covered city through the window and pushed the redhead from his mind. She was gone, and he had no way to find her. Now that he was thinking clearer, he should have demanded her real name, phone number, address, and anything else he would need today to get her back. He wanted her back.

His thoughts were interrupted by a knock on the outer door. Getting out of bed, he pulled on his underwear and pants to let Harrison in, the only person who should know where he was. Well, Harrison and now the redhead.

His buddy strode through the room and looked around. For what, Jonas didn't know, but he slid back on his shirt as his friend did his search. The room was semi-clean, after all. Looking down, Jonas saw a condom wrapper on the floor and quickly kicked it under the bed.

"Nice, Jonas. You're supposed to be lying low, not finding someone to fuck." Harrison was holding the tank top that the redhead had worn the night before. He has missed the fact that she had forgotten that.

"Can't help that the ladies love me." Jonas grabbed the shirt away from him, happy that she wasn't here when his lawyer showed up. Harrison had never given him any indication that he had ever hooked up with a stranger in a hotel. He had been married for years and now was getting married again. Commitment was what Harrison knew best; Jonas had never been caught in that trap.

"They love the money you have, not the real you," Harrison stated.

Jonas wondered if it was true. The hotel he was staying at wasn't just any hotel; it was one of the high-end ones. She could have chosen any room and found someone well-off for the night, but he didn't like to think about Trixi like that.

"So what? I take every advantage that money affords me," he argued.

"You need to find yourself a wife." Harrison walked out of the bedroom part of the suite and into the living room.

"I don't think I'll ever be ready to settle down," he insisted as he tried not to picture the redhead from last night. Not that he would settle down with her but enjoy her a few more times? Yes. After all, he was still coming off an evening with his dad and Judith. After that reminder, he was never getting married.

"I wouldn't consider it settling down at all. Not this time. I was just like you after my divorce. Now I can't wait to make her mine." Harrison sat on the couch with a lopsided grin.

"When is the big day?" As if Harrison didn't tell him every time they talked. The man was so excited to get hitched again it was scary.

"In four days, so you should be happy I'm here today since I should be getting ready. You couldn't have timed this any worse, Jonas."

"Four days of freedom left." Jonas dismissed the timing quip to razz his friend.

Harrison didn't take the bait. "It's not freedom anymore after you've met her and then want nothing but to be with her."

"Why aren't you with her right now then?" Jonas asked. After all, brunch had been Harrison's idea, not Jonas's. He didn't need a formal introduction to Harrison's new bride. Harrison had all but insisted on it.

"Because I'm getting your ass out of bed so that you're ready for brunch with us. Sera and her daughters are having breakfast while I get you cleaned up and ready."

"Breakfast *and* brunch? How much does this woman eat?" Jonas teased as he grabbed clothes from his suitcase.

"It's a big thing with them. It's the only time they spend together sometimes, and since the wedding is this weekend, there won't be another time for them to get together. She promised not to eat," Harrison stated and sat on the couch, pulling out his phone.

"Still seems odd. How many kids does she have?" Jonas asked.

"Seven in total, but only two are mine." He shrugged as if every woman had half a dozen kids.

"Are you going to turn into an overprotective daddy?" He grinned at his joke.

"No need. They already have an overprotective mama. It would just be redundant if I was too." He laughed. "Now get yourself put together. Sera demanded that she meet you before we leave since after we get back from the honeymoon, it'll be a mess around you."

"Are there bigger girls? Maybe they should be at brunch. Any redheads? You know I love me a redhead," Jonas suggested, squashing down images of the redhead from the night before.

"They're off-limits. Even the redhead." Harrison's voice was hard, considering he had just said he wasn't going to be overprotective.

"Overprotective daddy?" He grinned at the man.

"Overprotective mommy. She'd kill you for going after one of her girls. I promised not to set them up with my friends. So, they're off-limits," Harrison stated again, not smiling anymore.

"Just make sure you don't miss the meeting this evening. If you do, Harvey will be on to you. We can't have you tipping your hand before we're ready. So far, I haven't heard that anything is starting," Harrison said.

"Don't worry; I'll be there," Jonas assured him but had completely forgotten the board meeting that evening. He had always attended, and it would look bad if he didn't show up. Except it was the last place he wanted to be.

There was no way Harvey thought anything was up; he trusted Jonas with almost everything after a decade of working at the company. Well, everything except the fact that he was stealing ten percent of everything that was coming in the doors—and had been for years.

Jonas had only stumbled on that fact last month, and it had been unbelievable. In fact, he hadn't believed it for a few weeks until the evidence was just too great. That was when he went to Harrison and the feds.

The company his grandfather had started during WWII had been at the forefront of investing in new technologies and had stayed that way until today. One of their biggest contracts was the government, which meant that his uncle was stealing from the government and had been for years.

He had wanted to talk to his dad about what he had found out but hadn't had the opportunity with Judith there. He would have to tell him before it hit the news. Maybe he could talk them all into leaving town before it happened, or at least his dad and his sister. Except it was probably too late for that since things would happen at any moment.

"It's my job to worry, Jonas. Harvey Raiden might be your uncle, but he doesn't want to go to prison. You could be in danger," Harrison reminded Jonas what the feds had said.

"Harvey doesn't suspect anything," Jonas said with confidence. His uncle has been stealing for years; no way did he think anyone was on to him.

"I hope not. Once I'm back from my honeymoon, we should know where everything is going. Sorry I can't postpone the trip, but I need time with Sera and the girls. I'm having Tyler Reed as your contact while I'm gone, but I hope you won't need him."

"I won't wreck your wedding."

"You're coming, though, right?"

"Of course. Wouldn't miss it for the world."

"Good. Sera's been planning this for years. I think she would cry if anyone who was invited didn't show up," Harrison stated and waved him off to take a shower.

In reality, he didn't want to meet this woman, even if she did hold his friend's heart in her hands. Right now, he had better things to do, like find a redhead that went by the fake name Trixi. He just wished he knew anything that would help him find her. Because he had nothing.

CHAPTER FOUR

"No eating anything, Violet. We're meeting Dad's friend, Jonas, for brunch," Sera Lovely told the eight-year-old on the stool at the island, as if the little girl cared at all about who the man was.

Jonas. Even his name sent Buzz's body into lust mode that morning. But then again, it had been less than twelve hours since she'd had the best sex of her life with him. She could still feel his hands all over her body; then there was his mouth.

He was probably the reason she was just sitting in the kitchen on a stool like a lump, unable to even pretend to be a part of the conversation. So, she just let her sisters talk around her. Buzz had six sisters and a stepmom, and they didn't even notice.

"So, you're finally seeing the client?" Harper asked as she pulled divine-smelling cinnamon rolls from the oven. Harper was almost always making something, but Lucy always made the cinnamon rolls.

"Yes. He's in a hotel for the week, and Harrison wants us to meet him before the wedding. Something about him being his best friend once. He's invited to the wedding also," Sera said with a grin, mostly at the cinnamon rolls, but maybe a little at the stuffed pork chops Harper took out next. Or maybe because in a few days, she would be married to the man she was so in love with. It was mostly that—Sera hadn't stopped smiling in months, and it was all because of Harrison.

Seraphina had married Buzz's dad years before when the woman was just nineteen and pregnant. Bradford Lovely had split almost instantly, leaving the woman behind with five girls ranging in age from ten to fifteen, never looking back. So, the woman Buzz considered her mom was only ten years older than her.

"Pork chop?" Harper asked her stepmom, who was eyeing them. Buzz knew the only thing Sera would miss about living in the house full-time with her five stepdaughters were the leftovers from catering jobs. Since Harper and Lucy had started it three years before, the family had been eating very well.

"No, Harps. We're going to brunch," Sera protested, not looking at the blonde but at the food on the pan in front of her.

"Are you sure?" Harper dropped one on a plate and pushed it over to Sera.

"Sera, are you enjoying your last days of sweet freedom?" Maby asked from another stool that earned her a side-hug from Sera.

Buzz's sister had gotten married not two months before, beating her stepmother to the alter.

Since then, Harper had also fallen in love and gotten married a few weeks before. Each of her stepdaughter's weddings had been Sera's way of having practice weddings. Each had made the woman change her actual wedding just a little, which meant no doves and no limos anymore, and definitely no Christmas decorations despite the wedding being in December.

"Where's Lucy?" Sera asked Maby since they were twins.

"Not my sister's keeper. I don't even live here." Maby took a roll from her sister and yelped as she burned her fingers on it, then licked the hot icing from her fingers.

Maby sucked on her burned fingers and looked around the room with sadness in her eyes. She had recently moved into a large house across town with her husband, a house everyone knew that Maby hated, which caused her to miss the Lovely house even more. But she loved Cliff, so she said nothing, though Buzz was sure Cliff knew as well.

Harper had followed suit not a week later, moving in with her fiancé, a man who happened to be Sera's brother and now lived near Maby and Cliff. So far, she was happier with the move, but she still worked out of the Lovely kitchen for her catering business, so she was home a lot.

Both would return to the house every Saturday morning for breakfast, an accidental ritual that had caused everyone to return home for years. Though until recently, it was from dates and not living arrangements. So, Saturday mornings were designated sister time. Or Thursday, as today was.

"Buzzy, do you know?" Sera turned her attention to her.

"Her door was open. I don't know." It was open at 2 a.m. when she came home and had still been open that morning. She could have slept there because Lucy hadn't. Both Harper's and Maby's beds might have been open also, but they sometimes stayed over the night before breakfast. So instead, she had slept on the couch in the living room, which was why she was up so early this morning. Harper's mixer was as loud as a freight train.

She desperately wanted to be cocooned under the covers and sleeping, letting her body recover from the multiple orgasms from the night before. But no, she was here, talking to all these people. So many people.

"Buzz, where were you yesterday that you couldn't help out?" Harper asked, putting a roll on a plate and handing it to Sera's eight-year-old, Violet. Sometimes, Mom was ignored.

"I was working on a story."

"Did you get it?" Sera asked in excitement, turning her blue gaze toward her.

"No, I just kind of messed it up. I'll probably get fired for it before you even get married, Sera," Buzz admitted as she got up and grabbed a cinnamon roll and took a big bite of the pastry. Really, she didn't want to talk about it. She wasn't a bad reporter; she just couldn't get any good stories. It had been her last chance, and it was gone.

"What are you going to do now?" Maby asked, not even trying to pretend to be optimistic. She was a literature professor at the university. Maby would never know what it was like to be fired—she was too perfect for that.

"I don't know, buy a paper and start looking for a job? Any openings for a liberal arts degree anywhere?" She plopped down on a chair at the table.

"Let me look for something. I have nothing else going on. I took this entire week off for Sera," Maby said from her stool, which earned herself a smile from their stepmom.

"Remember, I have no experience in anything," Buzz pointed out from the table.

"You have a little experience in everything," Sera argued as she finally grabbed the plate of pork chops from Harper. Sera loved it there. She also didn't let her kids get down on themselves. Her glass was always full and running over.

"Thanks, Mom, but I've seen my resume," Buzz said.

"Okay, enough about Buzz's job crisis. She's always in one," Harper cut in as she chopped her remaining cinnamon rolls into squares. "So, Buzz, why were you on the couch this morning? You have a bedroom upstairs now that I've moved out."

"I forgot. And sometimes you stay anyway," Buzz mumbled. No way was she telling her that her brain was in an orgasm-induced haze when she stumbled in. "Besides, you two both come back all the time, and Sera hasn't moved out yet."

"I'm getting there," Sera stated, though her "getting there" was actually not happening. It was now four days before the wedding, and not a single box had left the house, though her new house was only two blocks down the street and almost completely purchased. They signed the papers the day before the wedding.

"I never stay." Harper folded her arms and glared at her.

"Last weekend, Kaine said something, and you kicked me out of your room at like three in the morning."

Harper smiled broadly, and her voice got louder. "He apologized."

"Not to me!" Buzz yelled back at her. "I'm waiting for Mom to move out. I want the master."

"Why is everyone yelling?" Agatha suddenly asked from the door. Her black hair was not combed, and she looked like she was still asleep.

"Buzz is trying to steal my bedroom," Sera told the woman.

"Ick. Mom's had sex in there a lot." Agatha grabbed a roll from the pan by her oldest sister, no plate needed.

"Don't care. I've had sex in this kitchen," Buzz said, pointing to the spot. Sure, it had been years ago and before the extensive recent remodel. Not to mention it didn't hold a candle to last night, but it had happened. Her mother's love life was not getting in the way of her getting the biggest room in the house with an attached bathroom. Well, second biggest room. Agatha had an entire floor to herself but no bathroom.

"Me too," Harper said and pointed at another location, despite her earlier "no-sex in the kitchen" rule, a rule Buzz was sure her oldest sister broke almost as soon as it was made.

"I can't even count how many times I've had sex in here," Maby said. "If I didn't already have an entire house, I should get Mom's room. I've already had sex in there."

"*What?!*" Sera glared at her. None of the kitchen talk had gotten to her, but her bedroom seemed to cross a line.

"Sorry, Mom." Maby gave her a side-hug, which Sera shook off.

"Anyone else? My bedroom?" she asked the room.

All heads were shaking, except Agatha, who wasn't paying attention at all. All eyes turned to her, causing her to look up. "What?"

"Did you have sex in Sera's room?" Maby asked.

"I have my own room for that." Agatha pointed at the stairs with her roll. "And a bathroom and a hallway, and this kitchen, and out in the living room. There are even cars."

"I hope you're disinfecting in here every day, Harper. Every day," Sera said, not turning away from the most introverted of all the kids.

"I am now." Harper also looked at Agatha.

"Really? Do you want me to point out everyone who had sex last night? I can." She looked around the room, and Buzz squirmed as Agatha grinned at her. Fucking sister with the eye.

"Go ahead," Sera said. Everyone knew she'd gotten lucky last night. She got lucky every night now.

"Quit bragging, Mom," Agatha replied and took another bite of her roll.

Buzz sighed in relief. Agatha wasn't telling.

CHAPTER FIVE

BRUNCH HAD NOT GONE AS EXPECTED. FIRST off, all the females at the table had already eaten. Harrison explained that the women had "accidentally" eaten at home, which was not actually a thing, to "accidentally" already have eaten.

So, the women just drank juice and mostly stared at him while he ate. He was starving. Good sex will do that to a guy—really good sex.

Instead of conversing with his friend and his family, Jonas could only think about finding Trixi again. That wasn't even her real name, so he had nothing on her. Nothing but a memory, a memory that made him hard just thinking about it.

Pushing the woman from his mind, he concentrated on Harrison's daughter, who sat across from him. She was the littlest of the two, since the older one was on her phone and didn't care about what was happening. "What grade are you in?"

"Second." Violet grinned at him. She was the image of her father. That his friend had two kids he didn't know about had been a surprise; in fact, Jonas hadn't believed it was true until he actually saw the children. They were Harrison's for sure. Nobody could deny that.

"What do you want to be when you grow up?" he asked, liking kid small talk more than adult small talk.

As she concentrated on stabbing a blueberry with her fork, she replied, "I am going to be a drawer."

"Artist," Sera supplied from across the table.

"Artist, like Ag," Violet added, giving up on the fork and popping the blueberry in her mouth.

"Ag is my daughter, Agatha. She's an artist," Sera informed him.

"Sounds interesting. What else does Ag do?" Artists usually didn't make enough to live on. If she was making enough, maybe he should look into her art and see if she was the red-headed one.

"She has sex in the kitchen and the living room and the bathroom and cars," Violet said, still working on the blueberries and not looking up.

"Violet, who told you that?" Harrison looked at his daughter and then at Emmaline, who was now suddenly paying attention to the conversation.

"Ag did. Everyone has sex in the kitchen." She popped another berry in her mouth and chewed as she finally looked up. Obviously, she got her openness and bubbliness from her mom. Until her youngest had started talking about sex, Sera hadn't stopped smiling.

"Violet, honey, we can't talk about sex outside the house, remember?" Sera chided softly, turning to the kid with no embarrassment whatsoever.

"She's getting kicked out of the second grade," Emmaline said from her chair, looking back at her phone.

"I am not, Emma. I'm going to be a third-grader next year!" the little girl yelled at her sister.

"Don't talk about sex, then. Adults don't like it. The talk, I mean," Emma corrected herself.

"What are you teaching these kids?" Jonas said as Harrison's face turned scarlet.

"Too many big sisters."

"I think I might want to meet these sisters. Violet, do you think I would like your sisters?" He wasn't going to ask the parents.

"Oh, yes," the little girl said.

"Which would I like best?"

"Ag. She is an artist and has her own floor in the house. You would like her room. But when the door is shut, you can't go in there." The little girl had stopped with the blueberries as she spoke.

"Is her door shut a lot?" he asked just to piss off the parents.

"No, not a lot, but sometimes. I'm losing my room," she added sadly.

"Who's taking away your room?"

"We don't need rooms at both places," Emma stated as only a teen could while telling her little sister something.

Violet folded her arms. "I do."

"Honey, if you stay there, you will have a bed, just not a room anymore. You will have a wonderful room at the new house. Remember you were painting it light blue? And Buzzy needs a room." Sera took the little girl's hand.

At Jonas's confused expression, Harrison explained, "Buzz sleeps on the couch or in an empty bed. The house is one room short. But now that we're getting a house, the kids will have rooms with us. It seems that the two sisters who are married are having a hard time letting go of their rooms."

"You're not moving in with her and all the girls?" Jonas teased.

"I don't want to live with six adult women. Well, four now, since Harper and Maby have moved out recently." Harrison grinned at his wife.

"That would be living the dream, like the playboy mansion. Do they walk around naked ever?" He laughed at the image.

"Almost never," the teen said, deadpan.

"Sometimes?" He looked at her. He might like her better than the little one, after all. Who couldn't love this kid with her dry sense of humor? So far, she hadn't smiled once, but her eyes said she knew she was funny.

"Three admitted to kitchen sex this morning. One was missing, and that one didn't answer the question." She pointed at her mom.

All eyes turned to the one who didn't answer the question. "Still not answering."

"That's a yes," deadpan teen answered for her.

"Emmaline Rose, stop."

"So, I'm interested in Buzz and how she can't have a bedroom. Why doesn't she get one?" Jonas asked the teen.

"She was the last one to move back. When she was living with that guy, Harper came home from France and took her room. Harper and Maby have moved out and still won't give up their rooms, so she doesn't get a room." Emma shrugged as if to say that was just how it worked.

"Where are her things?" He had no idea why he cared.

"There's a closet in the hallway," Sera said, giving her daughter more berries.

"Why doesn't she just move out and find her own place?" Jonas asked.

"What would she want to move out for?" Sera asked, her face showed confusion at his question.

"Because she's slept on the couch for two years," Jonas stated the obvious. Maybe Sera was confused because she hadn't been the one on the couch.

"Very rarely, Jonas. She only sleeps on the couch when everyone is home. That rarely happens," Emma stated. "And now she gets Mom's room when she and Harry get married."

"But she hasn't had sex in there yet. Just Maby," Violet added, which only confused Jonas more.

"Have you two ever thought about not talking about sex around the children?"

"Nope," said the teen to her phone.

"Are you ready for the meeting tonight?" Harrison changed the subject.

Six hours later, he was still thinking about the redhead in his bed and all the sex Harrison's stepdaughters were getting. Even though he wouldn't touch them, they sounded like great fun. He hoped that by the time the wedding happened, he would have the redhead out of his head and system. He was up for kitchen sex as much as the next guy.

With his mind on all that, he had managed to put his uncle out of his mind for a few hours.

CHAPTER SIX

"ARE YOU SLEEPING, BUZZ?" Maby said and forced Buzz to sit up on the couch so that she could sit down. Plopping down with her bag of chips, she took the remote and changed it away from the movie that was ending. Buzz had immediately fallen asleep when the movie had started, only to dream of Jonas Raiden.

Her mind had played back the evening before, and it was as hot in the replay as it had been the first time. Now all she wanted to do was to go back to sleep and be with him again.

"No, because you woke me up," Buzz grumbled and snatched the chip bag from her. Grabbing a few, she tried to make up for not being with Jonas with salt. She had basically wasted the day thinking about him, dreaming about him, and all-around missing him.

Grabbing it back, Maby said, "You have to be at work in an hour, and I am not covering for you today."

"I didn't ask you to, Mabel!" Buzz yelled at her sister. Maybe it was undeserving, but it felt right. Her sister shouldn't even be at the house —she didn't live there anymore. Why wasn't she with her husband?

"Harper is going to be pissed at you if you're late, especially after you ditched her yesterday." Her words had Buzz flying off the couch to get into the shower. No way was she not showering before working.

Harper would be pissed … again. Over the past few months, while Buzz had been getting her reporting career off the ground, she had not been able to help her sisters as much as usual. On Monday, it would be her only job, so she had better make sure her boss liked her.

Once showered, she put on black slacks and a ironed, white button-up shirt from Harper's room. After pulling her hair back into a loose bun, she shrugged at herself in the mirror: she was a catering waitress now. How many times had she worn that exact outfit over the years? Too many to count.

Back in the living room, she asked Maby if anyone else was going, who told her that Harper and Lucy were already there, and Agatha was on her way also. That surprised Buzz. Lucy hadn't helped all that much in weeks.

Maby also reminded her that she was late.

In her Jeep, she hurried across town to the address Harper had texted her hours before. She only broke a few traffic laws to get there only five minutes late, which was completely on-time for Buzz. Not so much for Harper, who gave her a look. Buzz wasn't going to let it bother her, though. No way was she getting fired tonight. Harper couldn't keep staff as it was, so losing her now would leave her shorthanded.

"You and Ag will be handing out apps. It's not a big gathering, but I'll be doing it too. We're short today." Lucy wasn't smiling as she handed the sisters trays piled with little, neatly organized food.

Grabbing the tray that held her favorite, she took one off and ate it quickly. The pure heaven of the perfect combination of spices and cheese made her moan. She said, "I love these."

"Quit eating them!" Harper yelled from across the kitchen.

"I have to make sure I can explain them perfectly." Buzz took another off the plate and ate it as she looked right at her sister. "And that they're not poisoned. I'm a life-saver." She ate another one.

Harper gave her a look and flipped her off. These were the same apps that were always served. They all know what they tasted like and could explain them for hours if needed. Buzz grabbed one from Lucy's tray and ate that one also. She loved making her sister mad, though tonight, it seemed she was already mad without Buzz even trying.

"Okay, ladies, be professional out there. No nicknames and no name-calling. No talking to people unless they ask you a direct question. And no accidentally dropping things on anyone. *Ever*," Harper said, mostly looking at Agatha, who was the reason for all the rules. Her reputation was built on her amazing ability to drop food on people who bothered her, and a lot of people bothered her.

"Is it just apps?" Agatha asked.

"Yes, dinner was in the boardroom, and Lucy and I did that. But now it's mingling hour, and we need more hands. Two hours," Harper said, holding up two fingers.

Groaning, Buzz was pissed. Two hours? Was it even worth her time for two hours? She should have skipped it and taken the wrath of Harper instead of wasting her time here.

Taking her tray, she turned to head out to the event with a fake smile. The room was virtually empty; most attendees were still in the board room. The ones who were there weren't interested in more food.

What Buzz had learned over the last few years was that there was one thing worse than being the lady who hands out apps: being the starving lady handing out apps. After her cinnamon roll for breakfast, she hadn't eaten at all, just lounged around the house, dwelling on the past and how she'd had sex with Harrison's biggest client and friend. By noon, she had put that thought out of her head and just called him Jonas.

More and more people came in, and Agatha gave her a look of annoyance that she returned to her sister. They had worked together so much that they had started to play games with each other years before. Each would pick out a person, any person, and they would pay extra attention and walk past them a lot. The other had to figure out who it was by the end of the night. It was stupid and silly, but it made the evening more interesting.

Her sights landed on an old guy who could've been her grandpa if she had any of those. He was her man for the night. She leaned her tray towards him as she walked past, and he took a piece with a smile —a smile that was a little too creepy for a grandpa to have made. Not looking at Agatha, she went in a large circle around the outside of the room, then a smaller one on the inside.

Other than the old guy, she paid no attention to anyone except Agatha and who she might have picked. After each round, she would slip into the kitchen and fill her tray. At the door, she would eat an appetizer and chew slowly as she completed her circles. She hated these events. They were so boring.

Agatha had picked a blonde lady in a navy-blue business suit; Buzz was almost certain of it. Her old man was constantly on the move and was not interested in her offerings, though he gave her a look at every pass. After another round, they were back in the kitchen comparing notes. Harper was off cleaning, and Lucy was loading trays with the remaining apps. The two weren't talking to each other, as was their new dynamic.

Neither had guessed right yet, so they headed back out, though they traded apps because it was fun to keep the guests guessing what each person had. It was petty, but it was all they had.

After another round, she realized her man was gone. She had lost. If your person left, you lost. It was a rule made early in the history of the game. Catching Agatha's eyes, she shrugged. The game was over unless he came back. Now that the fun was over, she slipped back into the kitchen, and Lucy took her tray so that she could go to the restroom.

Across the room, she slipped out the door and walked slowly down the hallway to where she had seen where the ladies' room was earlier. She needed a moment to herself, away from people, her sisters, and the memories of the night before, which were ever-present.

CHAPTER SEVEN

HER NAME WAS BEATRIX, and she was there. Jonas had watched her walk around the room three times before he had stopped another waitress and asked her name. The black-haired woman raised a brow at him but told him. At first, he hadn't believed her, but since she had gone by Trixi the previous night, he was sure it was her real name.

Today her red hair was up in a messy bun that failed to contain all of it. Red tendrils ran down her back to the white blouse and black pants she wore that matched the other waitress's.

Jonas sat on a chair in the corner of the room and watched her. Every time around, she had stopped or paused by his uncle. Harvey Raiden was very interested in the sudden attention from an attractive younger woman and seemed to get more and more interested as the evening went on.

It had taken him by surprise when the redhead from last night had walked out of the backroom with a tray in her hand. He had recognized her immediately; his body had too. She was just as sexy today as she had been yesterday, maybe even more so. Today he knew the sex kitten that was underneath the white shirt and black pants, and he wanted her again.

The two waitresses seemed to have a secret language and were communicating every time their eyes met. This wasn't either one's first time working together. The other two who were involved in the catering didn't seem to know the language.

A long-time member of the board had left, and Harvey had followed him, which was interesting. But then his Beatrix had followed them soon after, and he was determined to see what she was up to. Maybe yesterday had all been a setup, and Harvey was on to him. *Would he use a woman to do his dirty work?* Jonas thought to himself.

Out the door, he followed her down the hallway until she went into a room. A boardroom? An office?

Just outside the door, he caught up to her instantly when he said. "He's not in there, Trixi."

Her head snapped up, and he looked into those grayish-brown eyes that he had watched sparkle, as she came in his arms. He hadn't been able to get those eyes out of his mind all day.

"Hello, Jonas. Who is 'he'?" she asked innocently, like the night before hadn't happened. They were just having a conversation.

"Harvey. He isn't in there." Jonas stopped in front of her, maybe too close, because she had to crane her neck to see his face.

"I didn't really think he would be in the ladies' restroom." His eyes glanced at the door above her head.

"Do you work for him?" he demanded, dismissing the room she was going to go into.

"Who?"

"Harvey. Do you work for him?" he hissed, and his hand slid over her hip, needing to touch the woman. He hated that he had to touch her again.

"Never heard of him," she replied and bit her lip. *Was she lying?*

"You seemed pretty into him tonight." His other hand had her other hip firmly in his grasp.

She didn't make a move to push him away, "The old guy? Royal blue tie?"

"You were flirting with him pretty hard. I didn't like it." His lips lowered to hers, almost touching.

"He's not my type." Her voice was breathy as she licked her soft pink lips.

"Good," he said and backed her into the door behind her. It opened, and he pushed her inside. His hand left her hip, and he locked the door behind them.

They were standing in a stark white, brightly lit bathroom, and Jonas didn't care. All he wanted was to touch her again, have her again. Pulling her tight to him, he kissed her right on the lips. Her response to him said she had been thinking about him all day as well.

She moaned as his tongue explored her mouth, and he jerked her crisp shirt from where it was tucked into her pants and slid his hands over the soft skin that he could still see in his mind. Cupping her breasts brought another moan from her mouth.

"What are you doing here?" He needed to know as his hands unclasped the bra under her shirt.

"Working," she gasped as he squeezed her nipples between his fingers.

"For whom?" He squeezed harder, and she gasped again. Not in pain, but pleasure, he was sure.

"Sisters, my sisters." She leaned her head back and forced her breasts more into his hands. Her reactions were the same as the night before: fast and responsive.

His mind was racing. Was she telling the truth? None of the four looked alike.

"What's your name?" His lips found her pulse on her neck, and he nipped her with his teeth.

"Bea," she whimpered.

"Just B? Nothing else?" He bit her again.

"Bea, like buzz-buzz bee," she groaned, and her hands slid under his jacket.

"Beatrix?" he asked as his hands squeezed her entire full breasts.

"*Yes,*" she groaned, but he wasn't one hundred percent sure it was because of the name or his movements.

Pulling his lips from her neck, he looked down at her. The other waitress hadn't lied to him, but then again, neither had Bea. She was a Trixi since it was just another nickname for Beatrix.

Gliding his hands back over her smooth stomach, he undid her pants and pushed them to the floor. He needed to touch her now. Turning her to face the door, he rubbed her ass over his erection as he moved his hand into her lacy black panties. His fingers easily slid into her folds, finding her already wet and ready. She was as turned on as he was.

He held her tight to him with his other arm, and her head leaned into his shoulder as he slipped a finger over her clit and ran it in tight circles, causing her to moan and writhe in his arms. All he could smell were roses and grapes from her hair, the same as the night before.

Her body was limp and sated as he quickly undid his own pants and pushed down his underwear. In one smooth motion, he pushed on a condom and entered her wet folds from behind. The action made her gasp, but she didn't protest or try to get away. As he began to move, she cried out in pleasure and said his name with the rhythm of their movements.

With a hand on her hips, he set their pace. It was harsh and fast, and she met him move for move as her body clenched around his until he came hard in her. Both were panting as he slid from her, and she groaned as he did.

Spinning her back to face him, she nearly fell because her pants were still around her ankles. She laughed at herself as his arms kept her from falling to the floor at their feet. Her laugh made him smile—it was infectious.

In her pants on the floor, her phone made a buzzing noise. Her eyes went to them, and then she quickly reached for the phone. Jonas watched her read the text and bite her lip.

"Fuck. Fuck, I have to go." She put her phone under her chin, holding it between her chin and chest as she pulled up her panties and pants, buttoning them quickly.

"I want to see you again," he demanded as she worked.

"Fuck, this is not working out at all," she mumbled as her phone received another text.

"Beatrix, I want your number," he demanded again.

"I have to get back. Lucy just stormed off. This is bad." She unlocked the door.

"Bea, stop," he called after her, but she didn't.

Mumbling to herself, she left him in the bathroom and went back to the party. Or so he assumed since he couldn't follow because his pants were still around his own feet, and his dick was hanging out. In the time it took to right himself, she was gone from the hallway. Back at the party, he couldn't see her. The black-haired woman was there, as well as the blonde, but now it was just two, and the party had emptied of most of the attendees. His redhead was gone.

"Jonas, where the hell have you been?" Harvey stated from beside him. Jonas had been sure the man had left already.

"Restroom."

"Haven't seen you in a few days. Stop by my office tomorrow; we have to have a chat." Harvey was nothing but smiles, except he could be that way if he wanted to.

Pushing the gorgeous redhead from his mind, he had to get back to what was happening. No way was a woman getting in the way of that.

If she worked for Harvey, she wasn't doing a great job, unless it was just to distract him. Then she was doing great.

CHAPTER EIGHT

FRIDAY MORNING, Buzz dressed in her best gray slacks and navy blouse to get fired. It wouldn't have been the first time she had been fired in the outfit, and probably wouldn't be the last time with the way her life was going.

Maby hadn't found any jobs on campus for her yet, but it was October, and all those jobs were full for the year. Buzz had abstained from looking until she was actually fired, so this afternoon, she was going to update her resume before heading out for drinks with the sisters. They were having one last outing with their single mom.

Pushing into the old building that housed the Times' offices, she wondered if her mom's work needed anyone like her. Probably not, but she would send her a text after the deed was done. Or after the woman came back from her week-long honeymoon in Hawaii. Maybe by then, Buzz would have found herself something, anything.

Sitting at the desk she shared with four other people, she pretended to work as she waited for her editor to call her into the office. Yesterday she had promised an exclusive report that was supposed to be on today's front page, but she had messed that up so much the only words he had said to her could in no way be printed in a newspaper.

But maybe she should write it down; it would make a great story. Then she'd hide it in her underwear drawer, where it would never see the light of day. But she could read it on lonely nights and relive it.

"Did you get the story, Bea?" Grace Atwater asked from the next desk over. They were friendly, but Grace was a backstabber, so Buzz kept her stories close. Grace knew there was an interview, but not with who or what it was about. And, hopefully, she would never know Buzz slept with the subject instead of getting the interview.

"Nope, missed him. Just my luck," Buzz lied and turned back to her.

"It sounds like Meghan Murphy is getting to cover the senator's scandal from over the weekend. You should have been at The J on Friday," Grace said in a stage whisper so that everyone could hear.

Meghan was Buzz's arch-nemesis; she got all the good stories. Okay, the woman had no idea who she even was, and Buzz wanted to be a real journalist, not a tabloid one. The only story Buzz had gotten was her sister Mabel's wedding write-ups, fluff pieces. It had been all beautiful bride and handsome groom, but nothing meaty.

"Good for her," Buzz fumed. It didn't matter that Meghan Murphy got a good interview ... and all without hiding in a hot closet for hours.

Pulling her phone from her pocket, she was about to shoot her mom a text to find her a job when her name was barked from across the room. Allen Jasper sounded just as excited to talk to her as she was to talk to him.

Buzz slowly slipped her phone into her pocket and grabbed her purse. Most likely, she wasn't coming back to this desk. No way was she walking through these so-called friends after being canned. She wasn't giving them that satisfaction.

Allen did not get up from his desk. "Bea."

"Allen," was all she said. No matter what, she wasn't groveling for this job. It was so not worth it.

"You promised me an interview for this morning's paper, front-page worthy. Instead, I had nothing."

"I'm sorry, I tried. I really tried." She really wanted to keep her job, okay?

"You assured me you had a friend of a friend, and it was big. 'Slam dunk' were the words I think you said."

"Maybe I was more optimistic than I should have been," she admitted, not sitting down.

Allan shook his head. "I need to have people on staff who actually write more than two or three articles a week. More than fluff pieces."

"I had that exclusive about the Lovely-Scott wedding and the Lovely-Hawthorn wedding. That was me." And it might have been a better storyline if she had known they were both getting married within a few weeks of each other when she had written the first article. But no, her sisters seemed to want to get married quickly, sometimes even too quick for the press that lived in their house.

"They were both your sisters. How many sisters do you think can marry well in a few months' time?" She wanted to say all of them if their mom had any say in it.

"My mom is getting married tomorrow," she hedged, though she was sure nobody actually cared except her family. They were pretty excited.

"Do I know her?"

"Sera Lovely marrying Harrison Dean." She knew he hadn't heard of them.

"Nope. How about you focus on freelancing and submitting a few stories a week? Some might even be printed." Allan didn't even sound convinced that would happen.

"I think not. If I have any stories, I'll submit them at the Herald. I won't darken your door again." She stood and proudly walked out of the office. As she headed for the door, she ignored all the eyes on her —they all knew already.

Two floors down in the lobby, she stopped to talk to Chelsea King, who she had graduated high school with. They liked to chat about people they knew, but more importantly, Chelsea was the current owner of the house Sera and Harrison were buying this afternoon. It was down the street from the house the family currently lived in.

Chelsea had nearly demanded that they be friends in order for her to sell to Sera, which meant Buzz became her friend, begrudgingly.

Buzz got in line to talk to Chelsea. Though Chelsea loved to ambush her on breaks, Buzz liked to talk to her when she was working since the conversation would be shorter if there were people waiting to drop off ads or payment. Chelsea was the face of the paper; she handled subscriptions and want ads that walked in the door. There were a few others who handled it behind the scenes, but Chelsea did the foot traffic.

In front of her was a woman dressed so close to her that Buzz was starting to think she needed to update her wardrobe. If she was wearing the same thing as a woman twice her age, she wasn't dressing right. Maybe she needed more of a change than just her job.

Looking down, she realized that she had actually stolen her entire outfit today from her mother's closet. It would seem fitting, but her mother—stepmom, really—was only ten years older than her. On top of that, Sera knew what to wear; that's why her closet was used by all the sisters. It didn't hurt that they were all nearly the same size, except she and Agatha were a bit shorter than the rest.

The guy behind her unexpectedly slammed into her, and she slammed into the woman in front of her. On a positive note, nobody fell down. However, it earned her a glare from the woman, who turned on her.

"Excuse me, young lady," the woman stated as if it were all Buzz's fault.

"Sorry, I was pushed," she explained, motioning to the man behind her, who was ignoring her completely. Jerk.

"Well, don't let it happen again," the woman replied and looked her up and down, then dismissed her with a turn of the head.

The action almost made her laugh out loud—that was completely her sister Harper's attitude. Cold and aloof was Harper Lovely, now Hawthorn. Why the woman reminded her of her sister, she didn't know. Funny how she even looked like Harper would probably look in twenty years or so.

The line inched closer to the desk, and Buzz wanted to just leave, but Chelsea had spotted her, and now she was stuck. Chelsea would be pissed if Buzz didn't stay in line and talk to her, especially since she wasn't coming back. What she did for her mother!

When the older woman finally made it to Chelsea, Buzz was only half caring what went on around her. Pulling out her phone, she clicked it on to check what was happening when the woman's words caught her attention.

"Dr. Judith Rowley, R-O-W-L-E-Y," she stated loudly as if Chelsea couldn't hear her.

Buzz stared at the back of the woman's head for a moment. That was her mother's name! Not the mother whom she loved and had raised her, but the mother who had walked out of her life when she was four. The woman had abandoned her husband and five young kids without a backward glance.

Buzz had no actual memories of the woman, just the memories of the lack of a mom. Neighbors watched her and her sisters when her dad worked, and Harper made meals so the kids could eat. Nobody walked her to school on the first day or asked about her day afterward.

"What can I help you with today, Dr. Rowley?" Chelsea asked cheerfully. More cheerfully than Buzz would have, but Buzz usually took the bait when baited. Chelsea did not.

"I need to put in an ad for a chef. Mine walked out, and I need another," the older woman stated, the one who shared her mother's name. Buzz couldn't believe this lady could possibly be her mother. Then she went on to describe at length what she was looking for, ignoring Chelsea, who was explaining that she needed it to be short for printing.

The two spent the next ten minutes going over what Dr. Judith Rowley actually wanted in a chef, which was a lot. Buzz didn't have to be a sister to a caterer to know that the woman had higher demands than she would ever get.

Elle seemed to finally be satisfied because she was finally taking the older woman's money, even if the woman was still complaining about her former chef. Once the money was exchanged, Judith turned away from them to leave, and Chelsea called out to Buzz. She knew her real name and liked to show it off. "Miss Lovely."

Judith immediately turned back to the desk and asked in surprise, "Excuse me?"

Her reaction shocked Buzz. She had decided it was just a coincidence and not her mother, except the woman turned at their once-shared last name. Judith seemed to growl and hurried off towards the door to leave.

Buzz rushed to Chelsea and grabbed the ad they had worked too hard on and scanned it, memorizing the information as fast as she could, though there wasn't much since Chelsea had worked her magic and shortened the thing down considerably.

"How are you, Bea?" Chelsea asked, leaning in closer because they were friends.

"Fine, good. I have to go," she stated and rushed after the woman who may or may not have given birth to her.

She had to talk to her and make sure Judith wasn't who Buzz thought she was.

CHAPTER NINE

FOR SOME REASON, waking up alone again seemed strange. How had one redhead, who he didn't even know, weasel her way so much into his subconscious that he missed her two days after he had last seen her? Rolling over, he groaned. It had been a long two days.

Not that he had any way to contact her. He had called the caterer that had worked the meeting and was told they would not give out any personal information about their employees. That was even before he'd asked about Beatrix. The sharpness of the answer meant he wouldn't be asking again.

Now he was left with no way to contact her or even find her. As excited as he had been about knowing her actual name, without a last one, he was stuck.

Today was Harrison's wedding, so he had no way of using him to find the woman. Though he thought that Harrison was a talented lawyer, he was sure his friend would never actually look for a woman for him, even with information about the company she worked for. So, he hadn't even bothered to ask.

Hours later, he was working on his computer when his phone buzzed with a text from his father about having lunch together—without Judith there, or so his dad promised.

They agreed to meet up at the club his dad insisted on being a member of, mostly because Judith demanded it—more evidence that his dad never said no to the woman.

Walking into the dining room, he stopped when he found his dad right away because the other person at the table was in a bright yellow dress. Judith was there.

Rolling his eyes, he almost turned and left, but Louisa was there also, looking bored and playing on her phone. She seemed like she needed someone who wasn't her mother to talk to for a while.

"You're late, Jonas," Judith stated as she noticed Louisa was on her phone, then grabbed it from her.

"You're not supposed to be here," he replied. He was tired of being lied to by his dad.

"I'm here to meet with some friends, away from you and your father's 'man talk.' Louisa has a tennis lesson today." The girl took her phone from her mom's waving hand, slipping it into her pocket and away from her mother's clutches.

With her phone back, she got up from the table and hurried off without talking to her parents or him. Jonas understood her completely.

"Your friends are probably waiting for you if I'm late," he told her as he took Louisa's chair across from his father.

With a scowl, she got up and straightened her skirt before dropping a kiss on George's cheek, a kiss he didn't acknowledge at all. Nor did he say anything as she left, just took a drink from whatever was in the glass in front of him. It looked like anything but water.

"I thought she wasn't coming?" He nodded at Judith, who was still walking away.

"She wasn't until I was getting my coat on, and then she had to come with. I can't get away from her."

"You let her back in," Jonas pointed out.

"I wanted to see Louisa, so I offered for her to stay with me to go to college here in town. I love my daughter and want us to be close, but Judith followed her here, so I can't even get close to Louisa. It's impossible with Judith around," George stated as the waitress brought salads to their table.

"Almost everything is impossible with Judith around." Jonas looked at the salad and realized George had let his wife order, even if she wasn't supposed to dine with them. He was stuck eating salad for lunch.

George leaned towards him and whispered, "I've filed for divorce."

Jonas tried not to roll his eyes. "How many times does this make? Three?"

"This is only the second, but this time, it will work," George replied with confidence.

"I doubt it, Dad. You always give in to her. Ever since the beginning." Stabbing his salad, he knew he wouldn't enjoy it.

"I think I know how to make it happen this time. She hates being back here; she grew up here and has always hated it. Most of the time, when we were in Chicago, she didn't even come with me when I came back for family functions. But anyway, I'm offering her money—a lot of money—to go back to Chicago without Louisa. That's where she wants to be, anyway. And I will only pay for Louisa to go to school here." His eyes were bright, and Jonas knew his father believed what he said. However, Jonas saw some flaws in the plan.

"No way is she walking away from Louisa or her Mr. Money Bags. You're stuck with her, Dad. She's never letting you go."

"I can't take it anymore. But I can't do it alone anymore, either. I need help."

"I can find you a good lawyer. I can talk to Harrison; he probably knows dozens of them." Probably way more than a dozen. Maybe even one who has dealt with difficult situations like this one before.

George shook his head. "I have a lawyer. What I don't have is a backbone. I need to stand up to her, and I can't do that alone. I need you at the house supporting me, helping me when I need it."

Jonas speared a tomato and looked up at him. "No way. I can't live with that woman."

"Nor can I," his dad said, even if he already was and had been for almost two decades.

"But you choose to over and over again." Jonas dropped his fork, not hungry anymore.

"I want out, Jonas, and I need you to help me. If not for me, do it for Louisa. She needs to get out from under her mother's influence." George said the one thing that could get Jonas's attention. He wanted to get to know his sister.

"Judith isn't going to leave her puppet behind." Jonas cringed when he realized he called his sister a puppet.

"She's invited Ross Chamberlain's son to stay with us for a few weeks. He's attending the same college as Louisa, and Judith is hoping they fall in love. Or at least fall into lust so she can be the grandmother to the next Ross Chamberlain," George stated sourly.

"Who is Ross Chamberlain?" Jonas asked, though the name sounded familiar.

"Maybe you don't remember him. His wife is Nadine Sterling Chamberlain. You must remember Nadine." George smiled at the name.

All it took was the name to bring up images of the sex goddess that was the neighbor lady who'd liked to parade around naked with the shades open. She was the best thing to happen to teenage Jonas.

George continued on. "Ross Jr is a party animal and had been kicked out of three other universities around the country. The Chamberlains don't have enough money to get him graduated."

"Why would she want that at the house?" Jonas didn't even have to ask; he knew.

"Judith is trying to make a match. She wants him and Louisa together." His dad didn't hide his disgust at the idea.

"Poor Louisa." Jonas picked at his salad again. His sister didn't need to get involved with someone like that. Her mother should know better.

"See why I need you? Even Louisa needs you." George looked around the room.

"I will do this only because I don't want some pervert hanging around Louisa, not because I think you'll be rid of your wife anytime soon." That would get him out of the hotel, a hotel room that did nothing but remind him of a certain redhead that had him checking his closet all the time.

"Thank you, Jonas. Can you move in today? Ross is due this evening. I hate to have to protect her one night alone." George pushed his salad away from him completely, bringing his drink closer to him instead. It seemed his dad wanted to drink his lunch today, and Jonas couldn't blame him.

"Harrison is getting married today. I have to go to his wedding," he answered, but even he was seeing his way out from that one. No matter how fun Harrison's stepdaughters might be, it was still a wedding.

"A wedding? Isn't this the perfect excuse not to go to a wedding?" George winked.

"You're right. I'll get my stuff and come when I can." He got up because Judith was again lurking in the corner of the room, watching them as if she smelled a plan in the air.

Looking at her, he knew his father would be married to her until death do them part. He may say he wanted to get rid of her, but for some reason, he kept going back to her.

Now he had to keep a lecherous guy from his sister, get out from under a hostile takeover, and find the redhead. But at least he didn't have to go to a wedding anymore. Not that he wanted to go to a wedding, but Harrison was his friend. Jonas needed an excuse to not go, and one had just been handed to him.

CHAPTER TEN

CATCHING up with the older woman was way easier than convincing her to hire her. Not that Buzz could boil water, but she knew where to get food that a chef made. After all, she was related to two, one of which she still lived with since Lucy hadn't moved out.

Getting Harper to give her a raving recommendation had been easier than Buzz had thought it would be, but only because Buzz wrote it herself. No way was she telling her sister that she was going to be a chef to see if some woman was actually her mother ... their mother.

Buzz hit 'send' on the fake recommendation and resume she took straight from Harper's desk. *That will teach her to not give up her room and move all her stuff out,* Buzz thought to herself. Once it was out there, she didn't feel a moment of regret about the lie because if it was her mom, she deserved to be lied to, and if it wasn't, well, she wasn't a nice person anyway.

Buzz had told the woman that she could start on Monday. After talking to Judith for a few minutes, she knew she would have gotten the job with nothing other than being able to start quickly. The woman had hinted at starting that very day, but Buzz wasn't ready for that. Besides, Sera was getting married between then and now, and no way was Buzz missing her mom's wedding for her actual mom.

Pacing across the back room of the cathedral one more time, she watched Maby and Lucy, the twins identical in their blush dresses, fuss with Sera's vail. The room was full of Lovelys in blush, except for the one in white. Only Sera would have every one of her kids in the wedding, all except Agatha, who didn't wear dresses or blush. She was in a black smock dress and looked so uncomfortable that even Buzz thought she should just go home. Yesterday she had stated she was coming down with something, and Buzz knew she was completely sick today. The sweat was almost rolling off of her.

Buzz tried to avoid getting too close to her sister for fear she would catch it, so she went over the other thing on her mind: Jonas. Not that he wasn't always there, just a good enough memory to make her hot and bothered. She had hoped that he wasn't going to the wedding, but even if he was, there was no way he'd miss her. She was fourth in line by the bride; hell, she was walking up the aisle alone.

Dying her hair would have pushed her sisters to suddenly ask questions since she had always been known as the redhead—it was how they introduced her. Harper was the blonde, the twins were brunettes, and Agatha and the two little girls shared a shade of black that Buzz longed for today.

"Stop pacing," Lucy stated and laughed; it was usually her with the restless energy that was moving around the room.

"Sorry, I didn't realize." Buzz sat in the closest chair.

"Buzz is just worried that she'll be next and hasn't found a man yet." Harper walked over to her and fixed a few strands of her hair. Looking down at her, she said, "You're cute, Buzzy. Your day is coming."

"Shut up. I don't need a man." She knocked her sister's hands from her hair, then checked to make sure nothing had been moved.

"Not every woman needs a man, Harper," Emma stated, looking up from her phone. This was wedding number three for the girl in just over a month, and it seemed the sullen teen wasn't so much into them.

"That's right, girls. Nobody needs a man. We're strong enough to make our way through life as independent women," the bride added as she fluffed out the widest wedding dress Buzz had ever seen. When she thought about Disney princesses, this is exactly what she thought of. The words themselves didn't match the picture.

"Just relax, and you'll find the right one. Look at Cliff and me," Maby stated, turning to her sister quickly to make her dress fluff out.

"You stole Cliff from Lucy," Harper accused her sister.

"I did not. They are not attracted to each other; he is attracted to me." Maby pointed at herself.

"Maybe if you hadn't jumped him, they could've had their slow burn," Buzz stated, knowing that ganging up on Maby was more fun than worrying about sexy men ruining her mom's wedding.

"They aren't attracted to each other. Tell them, Lucy." She turned to her twin.

"I don't know. I think Cliff and I could have had a future." Lucy sat down next to Agatha, who frowned and scooted away from her.

Buzz was sure the action was because the words could cause a fight, and Agatha didn't want to be in the middle of it. An oddity in itself since she was usually very willing to fight at any moment.

Maby threw her hands in the air and headed out of the room, probably to see her husband. The couple had only been together for a few months, and Maby was still easy to rile up about it. It didn't help that Lucy had been against the pair in the beginning. Or at least when she found out since the entire family knew before Lucy did.

"I hope this lasts until summer. She is so easy right now," Lucy stated what everyone was thinking.

"Is there any way I can get married without you five fighting? I think I had you all sign a contract stating no actual fights two weeks before and until midnight of the actual wedding." Sera pointed at her suitcase that was on a table, which held said contracts. That's what happened when a lawyer joined the family. Contracts!

"Just having some fun, Mom," Agatha replied, though she hadn't been involved at all.

"No more fun; This is my wedding, girls. I've dreamed of this for years. My. Damn. Wedding. And nobody is having fun at my wedding! Wait." She stopped and went back over her words.

"Your wedding is going to be perfect no matter what, Sera," Agatha said, getting up and walking over to her. "I'm not going to hug you," she warned and took another step away from the bride. "You're marrying Harrison; that is the only thing that is important here. That you and Harrison finally get your happily ever after. Now just relax and enjoy everything that you've planned and dreamed of."

"Okay." Sera looked up at the ceiling as she said it, and Buzz knew she was trying to stop the tears from falling down her face and wrecking her makeup.

"Don't cry." Agatha scowled.

"I'm not," Sera's thick voice said to the ceiling.

Everyone knew she was. Even Violet brought her a tissue so that she could dab at her eyes. Violet was the only one in the room who actually looked good in the dresses their mom had chosen for them. Being a cute little kid helped.

Maby rushed back into the room flushed and happy, announcing that the wedding was about to start. Buzz knew the real reason why she was flushed. The fact that Lucy had to fix her hair, and Harper had to fix her dress meant that Cliff had convinced her he loved only her and that she didn't steal him from anyone.

As the concert pianist started playing the "Wedding March," Buzz waited in the second-longest line she had been in this week. First up was Emma, who had somehow hidden her phone in her cleavage, which Buzz had just noticed she had when they were trying on dresses weeks ago. *When had that happened?* Emma had a bigger chest than Buzz did! Then it was her turn since they were going in order of age.

Buzz half expected murmurs to start once she stepped into the room, but she was met with near silence. All eyes were on her, but her eyes were focused on the priest in front of the room. Next to him was Harrison, who was just watching his kid in front of her.

Buzz was happy he had taken on the dad role with gusto. She'd been surprised when she had found out that he was not only Violet's dad but Emma's as well. It seemed that Sera had met him twice over the course of her life and happened to get knocked up both times—then hidden the fact for two different reasons.

But since he'd found out, he had been the best dad ever: taking them places, having the three all stay overnight at his place, and buying a house with Sera that she, not him, exactly, loved. All because he wanted to make sure the kids were happy. He wasn't even rushing the kids to move from the house they had been raised in. Or Sera, for that matter.

After the honeymoon, the big sisters would have to force Sera to move in with her husband and take her kids with her since the new house was theirs as of yesterday. Even Buzz could see that Sera was never moving on her own. She had one excuse after another about not doing it.

At the front of the cathedral, she turned and scanned the attendance for one face. For the entire time the twins and Harper slowly walked up the aisle, she looked but didn't see him.

A rush of relief washed through her, followed instantly by disappointment that he wasn't there. She admitted to herself that she wanted to see him again. As her mind flashed back to her time with him, she was nearly too distracted to watch Sera float down the aisle behind Violet.

Nobody could deny that all her planning was paying off; nothing was left to chance, and it was perfect. From the vows, right through the dance to the happy couple being taken away in a horse-drawn carriage at midnight, everything was all Sera.

Once the hoofs clip-clopped away, she and Agatha gathered up Violet and Emma and headed home. The day had been exhausting. Both kids had fallen asleep in the car, as had she, which was okay because Agatha drove. Not much was said as everyone shuffled to their bedrooms. Buzz took Harper's that night. With how Kaine was looking at her all day, there was no way she was coming home. When and if Lucy came home, Buzz didn't know.

By noon the next day, Harrison and Sera were back and dressed like normal people and picking up the girls and their suitcases to head out for their honeymoon. The plane was leaving in the afternoon, and it was all Harrison had wanted from the wedding: time with his family. The trip was all him, which involved tears from his new bride as she said goodbye to the two women who were in the house and awake: Buzz and Agatha.

Once the front door closed, she started to get ready to start her career as a chef—or a fake chef, because she was never going to be a real one. Then she had a week to find out if Dr. Judith Rowley was the same woman that had walked away forever from the same kids Sera barely could leave for a week.

Telling herself it didn't matter didn't stop Buzz from needing to know.

CHAPTER ELEVEN

STAYING at his father's house was nearly impossible!

Judith was intolerable, and her house guests were even worse. One had turned quickly into two when Ross Chamberlain Jr had brought his friend Brett Andrews with him.

Ross was an obnoxious kid who didn't care what anyone thought about him, but Brett wasn't from money. It also turned out that Ross didn't care a bit about Louisa, but Brett seemed to be very interested in Jonas's blonde-haired little sister. Everything he said made her giggle like a schoolgirl, which she was, but some college kid shouldn't make her do that.

This sudden need to protect his sister was new and a complete surprise to Jonas. They had never been close, but here he was, wanting to kick both men from the house because neither dared to talk to his sister.

Which was why he was staying at his dad's house right now, as his baby sister watched a chick flick in a tank top she shouldn't have been able to wear until she could buy alcohol. Ross was out of the house or at least not in the den, but Brett was practically sitting on top of his sister. His dad had been right to worry, even if the guy he was worried about wasn't the one who was leering at his daughter.

"Jonas, can you get us some snacks?" Louisa asked him innocently —too innocently, in his mind. He was watching the stupid movie from the most uncomfortable side chair ever and was enjoying it, or so he pretended.

Before he could answer, Brett added, "And drinks, man."

He got up from the chair in a huff, sure that the kid's hands would be all over his sister the moment he left. It was what he would have done in the same situation. But of course, he had been a pervert at that age also.

Hurrying out of the room because he wasn't leaving them alone long enough for anything, he headed to the kitchen. Today, Judith had actually found a chef who would work for her. No more take-out for his stepmother. Not that he cared; he would eat anything.

"Jonas, come and meet the new chef," Judith called to him the moment he entered the kitchen.

Jonas rolled his eyes. He hadn't wanted or needed to meet the person who managed the food. If the chef withheld the snacks, on the other hand, then there would be war.

Looking from his stepmother to the woman in the white coat, he stopped breathing. Beatrix in the flesh. Her red hair was tied up in a tight bun on the top of her head, and she was staring at him like he was an alien. He was sure he was looking at her the same way.

"Bea Bradford, this is my son, Jonas." She indicated to him.

The redhead looked from him to Judith and back again. Her face had gone completely pale under the splattering of freckles across her nose. "Son? How old are you?"

"That's impolite to ask, dear. Where are your manners? Didn't your parents teach you anything? He's not my real son, just my step-son. I'm not nearly old enough to have a child his age, but I've been married to his father for years now. I raised him," Judith stated as if she'd done anything special for him over the years.

He had been thwarted in all attempts to find her, but now she was here, right in the same house as him. Taking her hand in his, he couldn't not caress the small warm hand as he did. "Bea, it's a pleasure to meet you."

Instantly, she pulled her hand from his and tucked it into the pocket of her white jacket. "Nice to meet you also, Jonas Raiden."

"The pleasure is all mine." He went into the pantry and grabbed a few bags of chips. No matter who was in the kitchen, his sister was alone in the den with Mr. Handsy.

"Ignore him, Miss Bradford. Remember, you have a clause in your contract about fraternizing with the household members," Judith said more to Bea, but it was also to him.

"Are you living here, Bea?" Jonas asked in case he wanted to find her later. And he did.

"She is not. There is no need for that. I do not need to provide a home for the staff, Jonas," Judith answered for her, just like she did for Louisa all the time, though he was sure that Beatrix was more vocal than his sister was.

"But what if I need someone to make me a midnight snack? Who will make that for me?" His eyes were on the redhead only; his words were only for her.

Judith huffed. "Quit flirting, Jonas. It's unbecoming of you."

"Let's ask the chef, Judith. Is it working?" He stepped closer to Buzz.

Buzz stiffened. "It is not, sir."

"Is B an initial or like a bee, buzz-buzz?" he asked, watching her lick her lips. He was sure her mind went right back to that bathroom a few days before, just like his had.

"Buzz-buzz," she whispered.

"I like it, buzz-buzz." He looked at her unflattering coat but only saw the body beneath it.

"We have menus to go over," Judith stated loudly. "You must leave the room, Jonas."

After grabbing two sodas, he headed back into the den. It wasn't very far from the kitchen, but it was long enough that he had time to realize how lucky he was with that woman. She was right where he was so often, and always just as surprised to see him as he was to see her.

She might be a good actress, but not that good. In fact, she couldn't hide her emotions at all; her face showed everything that ran through her mind.

In the den, Louisa was no longer watching TV, unless she was watching from the back of her head. She was facing the pervert, and not just facing him—she was on his lap, and they were kissing.

Dropping everything he was carrying, or throwing it all, he rushed the couch and grabbed the kid by the shoulder, pulling him away from his sister. The kid's hands were so caught up under his sister's shirt that Jonas thought it had ripped as she fell to the floor.

Slamming the kid into the coffee table, it splintered under the force. All he could see was what the pervert had been doing to his innocent sister. His only goal was to keep her that way.

"Jonas, let him go!" Louisa yelled from the floor.

"In a minute," he mumbled as he drew back his fist. The kid shut his eyes, seeing what was going to happen and having no way to stop it.

"Jonas, what are you doing?" Judith demanded from far away.

Before he could punch the punk, something barreled into him, knocking him off the kid and onto the floor. Once he figured out what was happening, he realized that Bea Bradford had tackled him. Currently, she was holding his body down with hers, which was no inconvenience until she sat up.

Her eyes didn't meet with his, and she didn't say anything to him. That she had come to Brett's defense was confusing; did she know him?

"Miss Bradford, no need for dramatics. Jonas, leave Brett alone. You've been mad ever since he moved in. You're just a guest in this house, Jonas, so act like it," Judith chastised, then turned to Bea and added, "Brett just moved in over the weekend. He and an old family friend, Ross, are staying with us as they go to college."

"He was kissing Louisa," Jonas defended himself.

"She kissed me back, man." Brett sat up finally, realizing the danger was over.

"I kissed him, Jonas. Are you going to hit me?" Louisa stated angrily as she got to her feet.

"You're thinking about nothing but sex." He pointed at Brett, who was still on the floor. Jonas had been that kid once.

"Maybe I am!" Louisa yelled at him before Brett could defend himself, but her words caused the kid to smirk.

"Louisa May, do not talk about sex. Nobody wants to hear about it," Judith argued.

"Louisa May?" the redhead whispered beside him, suddenly staring at his sister. "Louisa May Alcott?"

"Louisa, go to your room. Jonas and Brett, clean up the coffee table. Miss Bradford, we have menus to create." Judith was over the fight it seemed. Apparently, she didn't care that Louisa had said she was thinking about sex, and there were two single men in the house not two doors down from the room she had just been sent to.

Getting to his feet, he realized that Bea was still watching Louisa as she left the room in a huff. Grabbing her hand, he pulled her to her feet. She was shorter than he remembered close up, but then again, they hadn't spent a lot of time comparing height before.

"You have menus, Chef Buzz-Buzz." His words snapped her back from wherever her mind had went.

"Leave me alone. I don't know you, and you do not know me," she hissed and walked out of the room.

Except there was no way he didn't know her, but he did want to know her better.

CHAPTER TWELVE

WRAPPING her mind around the menus that Judith had given her was even harder than getting her mind around the fact that Jonas was possibly her stepbrother. Was it even a stepbrother if you never met him before?

After four hours in the house, she was almost ninety-five percent sure the woman was her mother, but not because of anything she did or said in the hours they had been together. It all came down to the fact that she had named her daughter Louisa May. Maybe the kid's middle name wasn't Alcott, but Buzz needed to make sure.

Who else but her mother would name another child after an author? She had been the only kid in school with the middle name "Potter." When she was young and would introduce herself as Beatrix, everyone would say, "like Potter?" Yup, Beatrix Potter Lovely. Bea Lovely.

All of her sisters had been blessed the same way, from Nelle Harper Lee Lovely to Agatha Christie Lovely. And let's not forget Lucy Maud Montgomery Lovely and her twin, Mabel Lucie Attwell Lovely. Maby was named after an illustrator and not an author, but they were an illustrator of children's books. Louisa May Alcott Raiden would fit right in, if only in name.

Based on the conversation and fight, she wasn't too much like a Lovely, who tended to argue and fought at the drop of a hat. There was no way Buzz wouldn't talk back to Sera, and if she didn't, Sera would worry she was sick. Never had a Lovely went willingly to their bedroom when asked.

If Louisa was a sister, that meant that Buzz was lusting after her stepbrother, who had almost kissed her in the TV room, she was sure of it. His eyes had been on her lips, and she had wanted his lips there. Contract or no, she would have kissed him back.

Jonas Raiden being there was a complete shock to her. She had given up on ever actually seeing him again when he missed the wedding, but instead, here he was. Somehow, he always showed up where she was working. If he hadn't been so surprised, and if anyone had known about this job, she would have been worried he was following her.

Tackling him to save the kid he was about to punch had maybe been a mistake. It was completely unplanned and shouldn't have happened, but she had to stop it. Though he had probably been right to protect his sister ... her sister.

Yup, Louisa May had been a complete surprise to Buzz as well. Judith had said nothing about kids in the house, which left Buzz wondering why she had raised one child but had walked away from five others.

When she had called Jonas her son, Buzz's mind had toggled between figuring out where he'd fit in with Judith having five more kids and realizing she'd had sex with her brother. Stepbrother was bad enough, but half-brother was wrong. Based on his age, she knew he was slightly older than Harper, who was the oldest, so it was possible. Except where had he been for a decade as Judith popped out one girl after another and raised them before taking off?

"Tomorrow, you will start with breakfast, correct? Then lunch and dinner?" Judith asked. Spending all day there was not what Buzz wanted to do, but she knew she only had to do it for a few days because she was not a chef and couldn't pretend forever.

"Yes, bright and early," she answered, looking closely at the woman. She looked a bit like the twins, but more like Harper. And nothing like her or Agatha.

"Good. See you then." Judith dismissed her with a wave.

With a shrug, Buzz got up from the table. She was ready to be gone. Without a word, she headed for the back door and started unbuttoning Harper's jacket. Judith had informed her already that the back door was the only one she should ever enter, which was okay with Buzz since it was easier to sneak in her already made meals through the back. All she had to do was get one of Harper's plug-in coolers, and she was set to leave the food in her truck all day. She had decided that this would be easier than she had originally thought.

Pushing through the door, she had the hot coat open, revealing a bright blue T-shirt underneath. A breeze hit her, and Buzz let out a sigh of relief. For days, the weather had been meltingly hot.

Before she'd made it two steps outside, she found herself pinned against the cold brick of the house, Jonas pressed to her front. His heat adding to hers kept the chill at bay. His hands were instantly under her coat and holding her tight to him by her sides, his thumbs caressing the undersides of her breasts. Her hands itched to touch the skin under the sweater he was wearing.

"Missed you, Chef Buzz-Buzz," he whispered breathily into her ear, causing a shiver to run down her spine. The fact that he knew her nickname was intoxicating.

"I can't," she answered back, but her body was pressing into his, demanding that he touch her more. It felt like it had been forever since he'd touched her.

He ignored her words and listened to her body as he ran his lips from her ear down to her neck, pulling aside the collar of the white coat as he did it. Her body ignored her commands to get away from him—she really didn't want to. She wanted to relive their time in the bathroom.

"I want you naked again, Bea." His hands were pulling up her T-shirt and skimming her bare skin, leaving a trail of fire behind.

"We can't," she managed to say as she tried to help with the T-shirt, but the jacket was blocking it from leaving her body.

"We *must*," he countered as his hands cupped her breasts, her bra no longer covering them.

Coming to her senses, she realized he still might be her step-brother. Until she knew for sure, he was completely off-limits.

Pushing out of his arms, she pulled her shirt over her bare breasts and stomped to her Jeep, or Agatha's—hers had been making a noise lately. Relief washed over her when she realized he had not followed. Her resolve was short-lived as it was, and she wanted to rush back to him and demand he finish what he'd started.

After slamming the door, she looked back at the house before starting the engine. Jonas was leaning against the brick wall, looking at her. A grin was on his mouth, his sexy hot mouth that felt so good on her body.

"See you tomorrow, Chef Buzz-Buzz," he called and waved at her.

She waved back and took off for home, which was only a short drive from the house that Judith lived in now. How had they never run into her before if she was still in town? And even if they hadn't, did she know what was happening with them? Did she read about her daughters' weddings when they were in the paper? Did she even care?

The Lovely house was completely silent. Was it possible there was nobody home? That never happened.

The kitchen was empty, and Buzz took a few minutes to gather together a few meals that she would bring the next day to the Raiden house. Happily, Harper had listed what was in every container and how to heat it up on the package. She wasn't called a control freak for nothing.

Upstairs, she checked all the bedrooms and found them all empty on the second floor. Buzz slept in Harper's room again for the night since she was acting like her during the day anyway. In the room, she hung up the coat, which now had a smudge on the back from the brick wall. The smudge mocked her for lusting after her stepbrother.

It was not quite 4 p.m., so she headed up to the fourth floor to talk to Agatha, who was usually up by now and drawing at her easel. But to Buzz's surprise, her sister was also gone. Her bed was made, and her room was clean, but she was gone.

Smiling, she said out loud to the empty room, "Good job, Agatha."

Her sister never stayed out overnight; she and Maby were the least likely to hook up with someone for just sex. Though Agatha had gone through a phase years before, she had mellowed now and wasn't as into casual sex anymore. Still, Buzz didn't know if Agatha had ever had a relationship either.

Back in Harper's room, she decided to try to do a little bit of research on dear old Mom. Typing in her name, she realized she had never actually looked up the woman. Judith had been gone for so long that Buzz had never cared about her. Sera had been her mom and would always be.

There was enough information online that Buzz didn't need to take the job to learn anything about the woman. She had married the head of the children's lit department in Chicago. He had recently retired, and there had been a write up about his wife and daughter, only named Louisa in the article, and a son, Jonas.

Digging deeper, she used Maby's passwords and found that Louisa M.A. Raiden was a freshman and taking a lot of English classes, with a splattering of science and computer. This confirmed her suspicion that she was named after an author. Though that didn't make it one hundred percent true that the two Judiths were the same person, just that the two Judiths had the same naming pattern. Maybe it was a Judith thing?

Buzz hoped it would only take a day or two to find her answers; she had no control over herself when Jonas was around. She just hoped she wouldn't sleep with him tomorrow and was only slightly happy she hadn't slept with him earlier that day.

But she was going cold turkey until the mystery was solved. However, giving up actual turkey would be so much easier than giving up Jonas Raiden. He was way yummier.

CHAPTER THIRTEEN

GOING for a run at 6 a.m. wasn't what Jonas usually did, especially not in the dead of winter. But he had to do something to keep his mind and body from thinking about Bea Bradford. A three-mile run should have done it, but instead, once he got into the house, he checked the kitchen for her and was disappointed that she wasn't there.

Once he was showered and dressed, he went looking for her again but instead, ran into his dad in the dining room. Since the man had a plate of food, it seemed she was there.

"Breakfast is on the sideboard, Jonas," George stated as he cut his bacon.

He didn't have to be told; it was supposed to be served from there. He could see the full warming plates and the smells that the food brought. Grabbing a plate, he filled it and sat with his dad. At least Judith wasn't there.

"Have you talked to Judith yet?" Jonas asked, though he wasn't as ready to be out of the house as he had been at this time the day before. Suddenly, there were so many reasons to stay. Or just one.

"I tried yesterday, but it didn't go well." George set down his knife and fork and pushed his plate away in defeat.

"What happened?" he asked skeptically, not liking the tone of his dad's voice.

"She's a very good-looking woman. Always has been. You must know that."

"What does that have to do with anything?"

"Just got me thinking about old times."

"You mean when you left her the other times?" Jonas asked but was sure that wasn't what he was talking about.

"Back when our romance was a bit forbidden, and we were hiding it from everyone. It would probably still be hidden if she hadn't gotten pregnant. I had asked her before, but she had wanted her freedom. After that, I needed the stability of being there for Louisa. It really brings everything into focus when your girl tells you she's pregnant."

"She was over thirty, Dad. Not a girl. How long was this secret relationship?"

"Over a year. I knew I loved her right away. We had great chemistry, but she loved being single and on her own, making her own way. She was very liberated before I met her. It was that woman I fell for."

"Are you staying with her now then? That independent woman you fell for?" If his dad wasn't over her, there was no reason for Jonas to be at the house anymore.

"God, no. I just enjoy having sex with her still. Can't seem to stop scratching that itch." George smiled.

"Not listening to you anymore." He got up and left the room. He was not listening to how good she was in bed.

Jonas headed straight for the kitchen to check on the new chef, who has become his new obsession. As he walked in, he caught her on her phone and so absorbed, she didn't even notice he was there. The kitchen was completely clean, and there weren't even dishes drying in the sink. If he hadn't eaten some himself, he would have questioned whether or not there'd been food at all. All he knew was that the food hadn't been cooked in this room.

"Can I help you with something? Did I forget something important?" She looked up slowly as she asked, no indication that he'd had her breasts in his hands just the day before.

"Just looking for the chef to compliment her on an amazing breakfast."

"Thank you. It was nothing." She actually blushed as she said the words.

"It was a nice spread; it wasn't nothing—unless you stumbled upon it and hadn't actually made it." His words made her bristle.

"When did your parents move to town?" She slid her phone into her coat pocket. He wasn't a big fan of the coat.

"Dad moved three years ago, and Judith followed over the summer. They're in a rocky patch."

"That's too bad."

"It's not. She's a witch, and always has been." He moved to get on the same side of the island as her, but she slowly moved in the opposite direction.

"How old were you when they got together?"

"Around fourteen, but she wasn't much of a mom to me. Not like with Louisa."

"She's hers, right?"

"Yes, Judith loves only those that she reproduces."

"Yeah, right," Bea stated, and her face went red at her answer. "Some moms are better than others."

"Yours is probably the best."

"Amazing. I lucked out completely. Well, all my sisters did actually," Bea said.

"How many are 'all'?"

"Seven."

"Are they all as gorgeous as you are?"

"Um, no. I mean, yes, they are all pretty … I guess." She shook her head and added, "How am I supposed to answer that?"

"By saying, 'No, Jonas, I am the most gorgeous of them all. They all say it to me all the time.'"

She laughed at him and let her guard down, but not enough that she wasn't keeping the island between them. It seemed her resolve to keep them apart was strong this morning.

Since he had to go to work that day, he would let her keep her space. Tonight, however, he would try a little harder. No matter what, she was still going to be on his mind.

Harrison had said he should try and go in every day like normal this week since neither of them knew when the feds were coming. Jonas hoped it was soon. He was tired of being on edge.

By evening when she served them chicken in a sauce with baby red potatoes, she looked more tired than happy with her excellent meal. Any excitement he had surrounding her new job was completely gone.

Tonight, it was a full table, meaning the entire six from the household since the boys had chosen to stay in. Brett and Louisa kept looking at each other, which was awkward since Jonas sat between them. Ross seemed more interested in his phone than those in the room.

Conversation was left to Judith, and Jonas was completely ignoring her that night. All he knew was that she was going from person to person, trying to get information from them, but only getting one-word answers. Even Louisa wasn't talking too much to her mom. George was completely silent again tonight. This meal couldn't get done soon enough.

Bea spent the meal flittering in and out of the room with more dishes or things that people had requested. From butter to more beverages. She was nothing but fake smiles; he had seen the real thing, and this was not it.

He tried to touch her when she was close, but she kept her distance from him. Though he had caught Ross grabbing her butt as she took his empty plate from him, and she had pushed him away and then avoided him even more than she was avoiding Jonas. At least he knew she wanted his touches.

Maybe he could interest her in a nightcap that evening. Maybe one in his room; then she wouldn't have to waste her time going home.

"Jonas, how was work today?" George actually spoke.

Surprised, he looked at the old man and smiled. "Good, like always."

"Boring, though, right?" Judith asked. She always said that.

"No, I love my job. Just because you haven't worked in years doesn't mean others haven't."

"I've been raising my children," Judith defended herself.

"Who are all adults. Maybe you should go back to work. What was it you did again?" He saw Bea crack a smile as she poured his father more water. She liked his joke.

"I have a doctorate, Jonas. I can get a job at any moment."

"I would like to see that. Have you regaled Bea on your accomplishments? Or Brett and Ross? I think they would be hard-pressed to be interested in your forty-year-old doctorate."

"Quit talking to the staff, Jonas. And it is only half that old!" Judith stated, and Bea headed for the kitchen, her expression unreadable.

"I can talk to anyone I want to."

"Just leave the staff alone. Bea is on thin ice after yesterday as it is." Judith watched her go as well.

"What happened yesterday?" George looked up and asked.

"She was flirting with Jonas. It was sickening," Judith told her husband but shot Jonas daggers.

"She wasn't flirting with me; I was flirting with her," Jonas argued. It had been him flirting; even he knew that.

"Don't flirt with the staff, Jonas," George said and turned back to his plate.

"You too?" he demanded of his father and got up and left the room. He was tired of the entire thing.

Not to be deterred, he went back downstairs an hour later, the back ones that ended in the kitchen this time. No need for his dad or stepmom to see him. But when he got there, the kitchen was completely clean, and she was gone. Outside, her vehicle was gone as well. He had missed her. Now he had to wait another day, but maybe she would have lost her control by then. Bea not in control was what he wanted.

CHAPTER FOURTEEN

ONCE AGAIN, she'd made it through the entire day without jumping Jonas's bones. Mostly because he had been out of the house for nearly all of it. If he had cornered her again, she wouldn't have made it, not at all.

If he had found her in the kitchen at breakfast, the entire family probably would have heard them having sex one room away. No way would she be able to be quiet with him. Twice he'd shown her what it would be like.

For another day, Lucy was staying at Maby and Cliff's place. Harper and Kaine had taken off on vacation for a few days, which was completely unlike Harper, but they were coming back tomorrow. Agatha was once again not home at all. A quick text said she was staying with friends, which was code for "she was hooking up with someone."

For the second day, the empty house was freaking Buzz out. If she wasn't hiding what she was doing from her sisters, she would have moved in with Cliff and Maby also. She might anyway if Agatha never came home. She hated being in the house alone.

On day two of her new job, she again took all the meals she would need for the day and headed out as the sun came up. As she drove, she ordered ten to-go meals at her favorite diner not far from the Lovely house. It cost her more to buy those meals than she was probably going to make during the week, but it was worth not having to actually cook.

Buzz used her shoulder to nudge the back door open and carried breakfast into the kitchen. To her surprise, Jonas was there to take some of the trays from her.

Totally busted!

"Did you order these?" He looked at the white take-out containers.

"No, I made them at home. These are just what I bring them over in. No need to get here an hour earlier than I have to," she lied.

"Good planning. I wish I could spend less time here."

"You can always move out." She didn't need to mention she knew he already had a place in town as she led him into the dining room and turned on the warmers.

"Not until those two shitheads move away. Ross and Brett are not going to be unchaperoned in this house." He handed her another container.

"I think Louisa is old enough to be around boys, Jonas," Buzz replied, though she didn't seem mature when her mom was around.

"Not these two."

"You're just being overprotective. She's an adult and has to learn how to take care of herself, though it is sweet of you to want to protect her."

"She can learn how to take care of herself in the wild. At home, she should be safe."

"I don't think she's in any danger, really. Making out with a boy is something all teenagers do. If she's anything like me, she's already done all that." God, she hoped her sister was a little less like her than the rest of her actual sisters. They'd all been wild and out-of-control teens.

"You didn't, did you, Bea?"

"Of course. It was a rite of passage. Drinking, sex, experimenting … that's what kids do." Buzz tried not to think about sex; sex with him, more precisely, because that was all she could think about.

"I don't like to hear about that, Chef Buzz-Buzz," Jonas's voice went soft when he said her nickname, making her knees weak.

"Well, I am an adult, so I have done all those things. You should know about some of it."

"I still think about you under me, over me, and me inside you." He snagged her body and pulled her tight to him. His hands caressed her as best he could with the coat on.

"Stop, stop, stop. I have a job, and you're not helping me with that." But her body didn't move away; she couldn't force it to. It was completely stuck to him like glue.

"Don't worry; she won't fire you. I'll make sure of it." His hands were expertly working the buttons of her coat.

"We're in the kitchen." Her words were husky even to her own ears. She was so turned on she couldn't turn it back off today.

"I have a room upstairs. Right up there." The coat hit the ground with a thump since her phone was in the pocket.

"I'm supposed to be here if anyone needs anything." She didn't move but felt his lips on her neck.

"Here works for me."

"No, we can't." Her words sounded correct, but his hands had slipped into her pants. Leave it to her to wear easy-access leggings when working for Mr. Sexy.

"Nobody will be up for another twenty minutes." She was sure he had no clue.

"I don't—" Her words were cut off as he picked her up and walked into the pantry with her over his shoulder. She watched her coat on the floor as he hauled her away.

After dropping her to her feet, he pulled the black T-shirt from her body. If it hadn't been stretchy, he would have ripped it in the process. Within seconds they were both as close to undressed as they needed to be. He had her wrapped around him as he pounded into her. It had been forever, and her body couldn't be controlled as the orgasm rocked her. Nobody but Jonas had ever made her come so fast and without lengthy foreplay.

"I missed this little body," he whispered, breathless as he ran his hands over her and slapped her ass once.

"We shouldn't have done that." She pushed out of his arms, and he set her down on her feet, which still had socks on them. Classy.

"Jonas, we're not supposed to have sex. It's against the rules and will get me fired. I know you don't care about my job, but I do." Which wasn't really true. She hated this job. She started pulling on her clothes as Jonas only watched her, still naked.

"And I said nobody is getting in trouble. Judith doesn't need to know, and if she found out, who cares?"

"I do! This is my job." Her bra was missing from the pile, but it didn't matter. She shoved her tank top back on.

Running her fingers through her hair, she didn't think he even touched it, but she had to make sure. Once out of the pantry, he didn't follow; he was still naked in there. Finding her bra on top of her coat, she grabbed it and shoved it in the pocket of the coat as she put it on. She would put the thing back on later, but for now, she had a job to do. Or pretend to do, at least.

When Jonas emerged from the pantry, she was already in the dining room, helping George and Louisa with whatever they wanted. They chatted quietly around her and didn't pay attention to her all. Even Jonas ignored her when he came in from the kitchen, fully dressed for the day and no longer in the running shorts and long sleeve T-shirt he had been wearing. When had he had time to change?

After breakfast, the entire group left, which gave her a break and let her organize the rest of the day's meals at her leisure.

Louisa was the only one who showed up for lunch. Buzz was about to put everything away when she wandered into the room. Buzz knew the kid was skipping school; the guilty look said it all. And it was only the second day of the new semester. As a woman who had skipped her fair share of classes, she knew a skipper when she saw one.

"Louisa, you're just in time." Time for an old-fashioned Lovely interrogation.

"Oh, I was just going to grab something from the kitchen and take it to my room," the girl stated, her blue eyes looking anywhere but at Buzz.

"No, no, sit. I have chicken salad today. Do you like that?" Buzz hurried to grab it. Louisa wouldn't leave if Buzz was making her a meal. She had manners, after all.

"It's okay." She sat down.

"How's your day going?" Buzz asked. Innocent questions would break down her defenses.

"Okay, I'm a little sick today, so I didn't go to my classes," she mumbled. There was no way she was sick.

"It happens. But does the sickness have anything to do with the male house guests?" Buzz set a plate in front of the girl and sat down a chair over from her.

"No!" her voice betrayed her a little.

"Boys are evil; that's what I've learned. Everyone always complains about women, but men are all hot and cold and emotional," Buzz commiserated.

"I thought he liked me, but then he didn't even know I existed." She set her fork down.

Bingo!

"Then he isn't for you. There are more men in the world than the ones in this house." Buzz should've taken her own advice.

"But he was so into me, I thought." Louisa seemed so dejected, like he was the only boy in the world.

"Hey, I thought so too. Every time I saw you two together, it seemed like you guys were going to make something of it," Buzz lied. She'd barely looked at the guy.

"Just like everything else in my life." The kid looked so dejected, so lost in the big world that she had no control over. It was something that Buzz knew so much about.

"What you need is a night out with your friends." Buzz knew that was exactly what would've happened at her house. Nobody was depressed for long there.

"I don't have many friends here yet, and I don't really like going out. Too many people … I'm not really a people person."

Buzz looked at the kid and wondered how she couldn't be a people person. Four out of five Lovelys were people persons, and Agatha could be if she tried. No way was this kid nothing like the rest.

"I'm your friend and would be happy to go out with you anytime you want to. I'm pretty good with crowds." Buzz grinned, but the kid wasn't buying it.

"I don't think so. I'm just going to go back to bed. I'm sick," she reminded Buzz.

"If you want to talk, I'm here all day."

"Okay, Miss Bradford."

Buzz groaned. How was the kid supposed to trust her and be friendly if she was just the chef in the house? She had to get beyond that with her because if she was a sister, Buzz wanted everyone to know her. Except Louisa wasn't like the rest, and it might be too much for a normal person.

At supper, only Jonas was missing. Handsy Ross was there to be avoided, so Louisa was all eyes for Brett, who forgot that he was into her tonight and just looked at his phone. It was painful to watch.

Leaving once the dishes were done, she decided she didn't want to be a caterer, ever. Once this little tour was over, she was done forever. No more cooking for her *ever*.

The house was quiet again; nobody was there. The quiet was almost too much, and Buzz dragged her blanket to the living room. After turning on the TV, she cuddled under the blanket and let the TV keep the quiet away.

As much as she wanted an actual bed in this house, she didn't want her choice of every bed in the place. It was too lonely without anyone there.

CHAPTER FIFTEEN

WHY HAD he thought that having a chef was a waste of money? He couldn't imagine what it would have been like without Bea Bradford in the kitchen.

At this point, he was planning his life around meals. Today, lunch was chicken salad, and he was just enjoying her fluttering around, filling his glass, and getting him what he needed. Nobody else was there today; he was alone with her.

"Sit down," he said for the sixth time. He really didn't need her waiting on him.

He should have gone to work but couldn't bring himself to do it that day. Just one more day without actually having to see his uncle was what he needed. Yesterday they'd had a two-hour-long strategizing meeting that was torture. So today, Jonas was home.

"My job is to not sit down." She folded her arms across her chest as she glared at him across the table.

"Get the contract and point that out to me." He waved a fork at the kitchen.

"It's so ingrained; it's not in the contract."

"Sit down," he bit out, tired of her excuses.

She rolled her eyes and did just that. She was as cute mad as she was happy. "Sitting." Was her snarky reply.

"So, tell me about Bea Bradford."

"Not much to tell."

"How long have you been cooking?"

"Years. I don't even remember when it started."

"Where did you train?"

"France," she mumbled.

"How long were you in France?"

"Three years."

"Did you like it?"

"Loved it."

"Why did you come back?"

"Family. I missed my family."

"Your big family, right? Seven sisters?"

"Five full sisters and two stepsisters. They are my stepmother's girls, and they're in school still. The rest of us are grown; a few are even married."

"Are you close?" Jonas smiled. He loved that she was opening up to him. He was finally learning a little about her.

"Yes. We all lived together until a few months ago, but then two have gotten married and moved out. But they're happy, so I'm glad they've moved out. The house is too quiet when everyone is gone, though."

"Where is everyone else? Aren't there still a few of you at home?"

"Mom took her girls on vacation this week and next, and Lucy has been staying with her twin. Agatha was out for a few days. It was lonely there."

"You could've stayed here. I could share my room with you." He smirked, liking the idea.

"Jonas, no." She shook her head and started to get up.

Taking her hand, he stopped her. "Can't blame a guy for trying to protect a beautiful woman. Maybe you need to invite me home with you so that you're not alone."

"No. Besides, if you're gone, who will protect Louisa?" she reminded him of one of the reasons he was there.

"That little twerp hasn't even looked at her in a few days. I think the near-beating was enough." Jonas was actually happy about that. He was tired of being on his toes, watching for teenage antics.

"I would doubt that. They're probably just going behind your back and hiding it. I have six sisters, and if she's anything like them, that's what's happening." Bea shrugged, not hiding her smile at putting that thought in his head.

"You know how to make a guy feel good, don't you?"

"Just calling it like I see it. How old is she, anyway?" Bea questioned, her fingers playing with the cuffs of her jacket.

"She recently turned nineteen. I wish Judith would let her be a kid; she's smothering her," Jonas admitted.

"Louisa doesn't seem to care too much about it."

"She hides it. I don't think she likes her literature classes, though her mom won't let her talk about anything else."

"It's just like ..." She stopped and jumped up from the table, rushing into the kitchen and away from him.

Staring after her, he nearly got up and followed when Louisa herself wandered into the room. Had Bea realized she was there? That she was coming?

"Jonas, you're home." Louisa stopped and looked at him.

"No classes today?"

"Not so many. What's for lunch?" She looked at his plate.

"Chicken salad."

"Again? It's okay, I'll find something in the kitchen," she stated and tried to walk past him.

"Sit. Bea will bring out something for you," he said. She must be getting something. He was glad she had known the younger woman was coming into the room, so they stopped talking about her.

"You need to keep your distance, Jonas. Mom will fire her. She's done it before. Do you want to be responsible for her losing her job?" Louisa asked.

"Judith won't fire her. She had a hard time finding anyone."

"Really? It took her four days to find someone, and mom said the woman begged her to hire her. Mom has something over Bea." Louisa looked at the doors to the kitchen.

"I don't think so."

"Believe what you want."

Before he could respond, Bea came back into the room with a water jug in her hands. Her eyes stopped on Louisa, and then she backed out of the room with wide eyes. Within moments, she was back with a plate just like the one she had given him.

"Sorry I wasn't prompt, Louisa," Bea apologized.

"That's okay, Miss Bradford." When she said the last bit, she looked at Jonas, probably reminding him to keep his distance.

"Anything else I can get you?" Bea asked them both.

"Can you get me some water and, uhm, can you take me out tonight?" Louisa blurted out.

"Of course. I know just the place." Bea rubbed her hands together and added, "We can leave at eight. I just have to swing home to change."

With that, Bea was out of the room. She forgot the water.

Jonas looked at his sister quizzically. "What was that about?"

"She's my friend, and we are going out for some fun. I need to get out of this house." Louisa pushed her plate away from her, then grabbed a chip and ate that.

"Weren't you just telling me not to get too close to the staff?" He raised an eyebrow as he asked.

"I'm not trying to get into her pants like you are. I'm just using her as a friend to have some fun," Louisa stated, grabbing another chip.

"Using?"

"Jonas, in no world would that woman and I be friends. We have nothing in common," Louisa stated firmly, getting up and leaving the room.

Gathering up the plates, Jonas took them into the kitchen, but Bea was missing, and the room was empty. Setting them by the sink, he waited a few minutes, then gave up. He would see her at supper anyway, and then she would tell him where she was taking his underage sister when she took her out.

CHAPTER SIXTEEN

From the sex pantry, she pulled her phone from her jacket and dialed her sister. Turning, she faced away from the spot it had happened, hoping she could forget it for one moment. Harper would help her out. Sure, she was the oldest of her sisters, but get some tequila in her, and she wouldn't let Louisa *not* have a good time. It was exactly what their littlest sister needed in her life—some big sisters to get wild with.

"Harper." Her sister sounded like answering the phone was the biggest annoyance of her day. Tact was not her strong suit.

"Harps, I need you to go out with me tonight," Buzz whispered, hoping that Jonas and Louisa wouldn't hear her. Not that it mattered, but somehow, it would seem odd that she had invited Louisa out with friends and no friends actually showed up. Harper was a friend of sorts.

"I'm married, Buzz. I can't date you. That ship has sailed. On top of that, I really am not interested in redheads. They have always been a disappointment, in my opinion. Then there are the laws that are against it. Not to mention that I have plans with my husband tonight, and he's already pretty excited about it," Harper rambled.

"You're a moron. Just have some afternoon delight right now and meet me at The Grog at eight. You owe me. I could have told mom what you were really doing with your boss months ago. I could have blown the whistle on that one weeks before it all blew up," she said to her sister in a harsh whisper. Her sister's job of being a personal assistant had changed to being more personal and less assistant. Buzz had been sure what was going on but hadn't said a thing at the time. It had all turned out okay, but things had been rocky for a while.

"All over, Buzzy. We're married now. Nobody cares what we do," Harper dismissed her threat.

"I think people care, and I have a platform to let everyone know everything about you. That wedding piece was a fluff piece." Since she hadn't told anyone that she had been officially fired, she could still use her reporting job as leverage when needed.

"Are you blackmailing me?" Harper sounded more excited about it than threatened.

"Yes. Drinks and a few hours. I have a friend who needs to get away from home and loosen up," Buzz stated, hoping that Louisa was *able* to loosen up.

"Is it for a story about someone other than me?" Harper demanded.

"Yes. Why else would I do this?" she lied. She had completely forgotten about a story on Jonas since focusing all her concentration on cooking and not fucking him. Both of which she was actually failing at, but it took a lot of concentration to fail.

"For that, I will help." Harper gave in too easily.

"Good, because I already lied for you, and you have given me a recommendation as a chef for a job."

"I. Did. Not!" Harper yelled into the phone, her breathing suddenly erratic.

"Already done. Thank you. And I have used your resume extensively," Buzz admitted with a smile. She might as well take all of Harper's wrath now.

"You are going to destroy my creditability! You can't cook. I have never seen you successfully make boxed mac and cheese!" Harper was nearly yelling at her.

"Don't worry; I'm using all your food anyway. You'll have to inventory when this gets done, so you'll have to tell me what I owe you."

"I want your first-born for everything you've already done. PS, stop sleeping in my room. After this, you are no longer welcome; it's mine. It will always be mine," Harper's words were rushed.

"I'll be out of your room once Mom is out of hers. I'm moving into the master, and I'm going to love my own bathroom. Just remember—tonight I am Bea Bradford and a chef," she said, unsure if her sister would actually help her out now. She was now on her sister's bad side, a side you didn't want to be on.

"Oh, like I can forget you're trying to steal my life. I have to go find Kaine to make sure you aren't moving in on him."

"Gross! He's my uncle." Buzz couldn't not say it since Kaine and her stepmom were actually twins.

"Do not say that. We are not talking about that. Ever!"

"Uncle sex," Buzz said, but her sister had already hung up on her.

Looking at her phone, she realized she shouldn't have anything to say since she was currently most likely having stepbrother sex. She suddenly knew exactly why Harper stayed.

* * *

DISHES WERE DONE, and everything in the kitchen was clean as she waited for Louisa to go out. Jonas had been at the meal, but Louisa hadn't, which meant that she would have to feed the kid also. No way was she going drinking with an nineteen-year-old on an empty stomach.

"Where are you taking Louisa?" Jonas asked from behind her. How had he snuck up on her?

"Just the usual place. It will be okay. My sister is coming with." She told the overprotective brother, not the guy she was having sex with.

"Which one?" he asked, as if he knew any of them.

"Harper. She's now an old married lady who can't have fun even if she tried." Not informing him that she was only recently married and that she hadn't lost her ability to have fun and probably never would.

"Then why bring her?"

"Because she's Harper. Come on, Jonas, she's Harper," Buzz stated the obvious. Or at least the obvious to anyone in her family. Harper was the perfect person for going out with.

"You make no sense," Jonas replied in confusion.

"You'll understand if you ever meet her." Buzz didn't have to explain it anymore since Louisa came down the back steps at that moment. Her jeans were ripped, and she was in a tight sweater. The outfit surprised Buzz because she didn't think the kid even knew how to dress. Most days, she was in clothes her mom would approve of, and this, Judith would not approve of.

"I'm ready," Louisa stated and looked at her brother with a frown. "He isn't going, is he?"

"Nope, just a girls' night." Buzz ignored Jonas's annoyance and walked to the back door, hoping the girl would follow. Because if he actually insisted, she would probably let him go with them.

Deciding to drive herself was the smart move—she didn't need the underage girl driving home drunk. It would take her more time, but it was worth it to know she was safe.

In the Jeep, Louisa looked around like she had never been in a vehicle older than she was, which was probably true. The quick drive a few streets over to Maple street was done in silence. Both seemed to have a lot on their minds.

Parking in front of the house, Buzz knew Harper was either at the bar or here since her new Land Rover was parked out front of the house. The bar was only three blocks away, so she sometimes parked by the house and walked. The car had been a nice little engagement gift from her new husband. It had even had the giant bow on it when he gave it to her like in a commercial.

Once parked, Louisa silently followed her into the house. "I have to change before we go. You can stay down here."

More than once, she had thought she should just wear what she had on for the day; nobody at The Grog would care. But she had spilled more than once on her jeans today. Way more than once.

"I thought you said eight?" Harper demanded from the couch. Her feet were on the coffee table, and she was watching a horror movie as she waited.

"I said we would meet at The Grog," she reminded her.

"I had to grab some stuff from the house, so I stopped." Harper turned from the TV and looked at Louisa. "I am Harper Hawthorne. The double H is still making me stumble."

Leave it to Harper to introduce herself and suddenly admit she was newly married, all in the hopes that the other person would ask about it so she could go on and on about how much she enjoyed married life.

"Louisa Raiden," Louisa stated but didn't move or catch on that she needed to ask about the wedding, the man, or how much they were in love, which didn't get her instantly on Harper's good side.

"I have to change." Buzz needed to get alcohol in both of these two before they wanted to go home.

She saw that Agatha's door was still open upstairs, but she didn't have time to see if she was home now. Usually, she called out to people when she wanted company as they moved about the second floor. Nothing today.

At her door, she found it locked. Buzz gave it one more try before she stomped back down the stairs. "My room is locked."

Harper turned from the TV. "*My* room is locked. I told you not to use my room."

"You said that nine hours ago, and I have been working since I talked to you. I need my stuff from in there," Buzz argued.

"That is my stuff; it's in my room. Take Maby's room." She waved a hand at her and turned back to the TV.

Through gritted teeth, Buzz stated slowly, "I need my stuff out of that room."

"My room," was all Harper said, not turning away from the TV, but she did smirk.

Without caring that a guest was in the house, she attacked her sister and tried to get into her pockets for the key. "Give me that damn key!"

Harper pushed back at her and pulled her hips from Buzz's hands, which meant the key was in her pocket. "Get off me, Buzz!" Harper yelled.

"Key, now." She pushed her further into the couch and sat on her legs, keeping her immobile. After a while, she finally got both hands in hers and held them above her sister's head. As she focused on holding both of Harper's hands in one of hers, her sister reared up and slammed her head into Buzz's.

Buzz flew from the couch to the floor, where she cradled her head. Her sister hadn't held back. *"What the fuck?!"*

"I put a bunch of your shit on Maby's bed. I'm going to take your friend, who also hates you now, to the bar and start drinking. Come or don't come, I don't care anymore." Harper kicked her as she headed for the door.

"Come on, Lou, let's get our drinks on. Tell me about yourself and your hopes and dreams, and I'll tell you how shitty Bea is." She said her name sarcastically, but at least she said 'Bea.'

"I'll be right there."

"Grab a shirt for Lou. She'll get hot in that sweater and will want something thinner later." Harper slammed the door behind them.

Half an hour later, Buzz walked into The Grog and was greeted by half the people in the room. Hopefully, nobody actually talked to her about her job. She didn't even know how she would deflect that.

After grabbing a drink at the bar, she spotted Harper and Louisa sitting in the back booth, which was her favorite spot in the place. They seemed to be getting along, which wasn't usual. Harper could befriend anyone; keeping that friend was her problem. She was too outspoken for most people.

Harper was a known pincher, so Buzz slid in next to Louisa. Setting the light blue shirt and her drink on the table, she ignored Harper.

"How's it going?" she asked Louisa.

"Good," the girl answered.

"You sent me drinking with a minor, Buzz. You know I hate that," Harper stated, though the kid had a drink—a tall, girly drink with a lot of alcohol.

That was why they choose The Grog—everyone got served. Well, probably not everyone, but a fair share of minors got drunk here often. Happily, the college crowd and the dead-beat high schoolers didn't go there. Just the regulars and their friends, and sometimes when needed, their little sisters.

"Did you two order pizza or something? Louisa didn't eat supper." She had forgotten in the wake of the fight to tell Harper.

"Popcorn, but I'll get something," Harper stated but only turned to the bar and yelled that she wanted a pizza. The bartender waved at her. "Ordered."

"So, what are we talking about?"

"Lou's big brother is trying to get into your pants. Now, I don't see it; the hair always makes you not as pretty as me, but to each his own." Harper actually reached out and touched a lock of Buzz's hair and looked at it in wonder, as if it wasn't actually the color Buzz had been born with.

"Did she tell you about the guy who was into her and then not?" Buzz asked, because that was why they were there tonight, for Louisa.

"Guys are shit; you always have to remember that. It's never you, no matter what they say. How old is this guy?"

Louisa sighed. "Twenty."

"Well then, he's not in charge; his dick is. Forget him. Never date anyone under twenty-five, and the closer to thirty, the better," Harper said matter-of-factly.

"She's only nineteen," Buzz reminded her sister.

"Which is why she shouldn't be worried about a guy. She has to spend these years thinking with her dick and screw anyone she can. When I was your age, I moved in with a guy and spent three, maybe four, years with him. Big mistake. I wasted my entire time in France on that man. I missed a lot of French cock." She took a long drink of her beer.

Louisa was just staring at her as if she was speaking French. Which to a sheltered kid, she was. Nobody at Louisa's house usually talked about sowing their wild oats. Louisa had a blush more scarlet than Buzz had ever seen.

Buzz nodded at Louisa. "Maybe tone it down a little."

Harper laughed and said, "Marry young, sex only on your anniversary, valentine's day, and both your birthdays. And never stray, Lou. That is the secret to a happy life. And you maybe want to put on the T-shirt. You look hot and flushed."

"I'm okay," Louisa argued, her face red from chin to hairline.

"Which one did you get her?" Harper asked Buzz, pointing at the shirt.

There were boxes and boxes of T-shirts at the house from when their sister Lucy had a screen-printing business one summer. She'd made so many mistakes that just went into boxes in the basement. So, if extra clothes were needed, you just grabbed a shirt. Not to mention that every one of the sisters wore the shirts with pride, mistakes and all.

Holding it up, she grinned. It said "WOL" in florescent green. The colors in no way matched. Finding out that Lucy had dyslexia had explained why everything was spelled wrong, but the mismatched colors were still a mystery.

Harper gasped and slammed a hand to her chest. "I. Love. It. I want it."

"It's Louisa's," she reminded her sister, who was already pulling off her pink T-shirt that said "D" on it.

Once topless, Harper pouted, then turned to Louisa and said, "Can we change shirts? I want that one so damn bad. You can either have mine, or I'll make Buzz give you hers."

Buzz looked down at her plain gray "Grand Cannon" one. Everyone at the house had the same one, and there were close to a hundred of them in the house still. Even all the husbands had a copy, but Louisa didn't know that.

"I'll take Buzz's." She pointed at her, surprising her that she chose to use her nickname.

As Buzz pulled off the shirt, she was surprised when Louisa did the same thing. Harper was happily pulling her new shirt on, and Buzz handed hers to Louisa, who pulled it on. She was pretty sure everyone in the bar was watching them, because they were two sober women sitting in their bras in the bar. And one that had just flashed everyone her boobs, as Harper had not been wearing a bra.

Odd as it may seem, it wasn't the first time or the last. It happened often with their shirts; everyone had a better one. That Louisa joined in meant that there was more Lovely in her than Buzz had ever thought.

"Nice shirt, Lou." Harper ran her hand over her new one.

"Thank you, Harper. What's with the shirts anyway? They're odd." Louisa took a drink.

"Our sister Lucy made them. She has dyslexia," Harper explained, though she was suddenly on edge. Lately, she and Lucy were not getting along like they always had. The catering business had been theirs together, but Lucy had recently stepped back almost completely to start a new job downtown that Sera had found for her. Since then, the tension between the two was palpable.

"Let's get another round here," Harper stated and tapped the table, then ran her hand over her shirt again.

CHAPTER SEVENTEEN

Jonas had tried to ignore the fact that his underage sister was out drinking, but it was impossible. Neither had told him where they had gone, and he hadn't been able to get to his car fast enough to follow them, which he had planned to do.

It was after midnight, and his sister wasn't home yet. Not that Bea would even have to bring her back just to sleep, but she should. This was her home.

A lot of scuffling and a giggling got him out of bed in an instant. Out the door of his room, he saw Louisa's arm about Bea's neck as Bea led her to her room, the one that Louisa was pointing out because Bea hadn't been on this floor before.

Rushing out, he grabbed his sister into his arms and carried her into her room—no need for her to stumble in there. Bea followed and closed the door behind them so as not to wake his parents or the boys, who weren't home yet either.

His sister was wearing a tight gray T-shirt, and she was still giggling. Setting her down, she almost fell, but he grabbed her to steady her.

"I'm okay." She tried to sound sober. "Just a little drunk." Then she giggled.

"I can tell."

"Next time, I want beer. Everyone drinks beer," his sister complained.

"Right now, you need water, at least eight ounces," Bea stated and went to the bathroom and filled a glass.

"I want another one of those drinks Harper had."

"You weren't supposed to drink hers. That's why she cut you off," Buzz said.

"Harper is Buzz's older sister, and she makes the rules. She said I have to loosen up and have more sex while I'm young. That I'm wasting time not having sex," Louisa proclaimed in a very series tone, then giggled again.

Trying to dissect the sentence, Jonas realized that Buzz was Bea, and Harper was her sister. It seemed maybe she was the wrong one to bring his innocent sister out on the town with. Based on his sister's new goals, he wasn't a big fan of Harper.

"No, she said you can't put your focus on one guy. Play the field, especially if he's not interested. She wasn't exactly promoting that you just sleep around," Bea stated.

"I kissed one of the bartenders tonight. It was a little gross, but I did it. Harper dared me to kiss a stranger. I think I'll do it again, but not the bartender next time. Another stranger," Louisa rambled as she tried to get her shoes off her feet.

"When did that happen?" Bea sounded shocked at the admission.

"When you went to the bathroom for like an hour. Harper dared me to do it." One shoe came off, and the girl grinned.

"Sounds like her. I dropped her off at home, and her husband was a bit pissed. But he'll get drunk sex, so he can't complain too much," Bea replied as she handed Louisa a glass of water.

"Anyone else getting drunk sex tonight?" he asked Buzz as they watched Louisa drink her water.

She flashed him an angry look, which meant it was a "no" for him. Because either she wasn't drunk or not drunk enough to go into his room.

Once the water was gone, Jonas found out that Bea was pretty good at undressing and dressing drunk people, making him think that the sisters might tie one on quite often.

Once Louisa was tucked into bed, she had to hug them both. Bea patted her an extra time and whispered good night to her.

As soon as they were out of the drunk teen's room, he pulled Bea into his room—there was no way he was letting her go. Her protest lasted close to three steps, but then she gave in.

It was easier to undress her than his sister, and he enjoyed it so much better. Finally seeing her naked again made him realize his memory was a little off. She was gorgeous in person.

* * *

By sunrise, Buzz was gone. But he knew she would be; she seemed very good at getting up in the night and leaving. After pulling on sweatpants and a T-shirt, he headed down to the kitchen in hopes of finding her, which he did.

But she wasn't alone. There was a blonde in the kitchen, who was making French toast while Buzz watched her.

"Did you at least give her a lot of water before putting her to bed?" the blonde was asking.

"Of course. What am I, stupid?"

"Just saying, you usually have a hangover."

"Not always."

"You get one the most often. The rest of us have some control."

"You were way drunker than me! You couldn't even drive."

"I could drive. I just let you because then I didn't have to drop you two off."

Walking into the room, he saw both women stiffen and exchange looks. Based on that alone, he knew Buzz had been talking to her sister about him. It felt oddly good that she was telling people about him.

"Jonas, what are you doing up?" Buzz asked.

"It's morning," he replied. "Who is your friend?"

"Not friend, sister. Harper Hawthorn," Harper provided, affirming his suspicions.

"Jonas Raiden."

"The brother then?" Harper asked, adding six more slices of French toast to the pan.

"The brother," Buzz mumbled.

"He's cute. Not Kaine cute, but nobody is. Doesn't look a lot like Lou. A little in the eyes, but she's a lot cuter all around," Harper said.

"Kaine is her husband, and he's not that cute," Buzz told Jonas and glared at her sister.

"You're right. He's fucking gorgeous. Way better than … this." She waved her hand at Jonas.

"You may leave now." Bea grabbed the spatula from the woman, who almost didn't give it up.

"I will, but only because I have to get to work. Nobody else in this family really works, just me," Harper huffed.

"Everyone works, you toad," Buzz hissed at her.

"Who is this?" Judith had somehow snuck into the room with them.

Both sisters froze at the words, and both slowly turned to look at the older woman.

"I forgot something at home, and my sister was kind enough to bring it to me."

"Tarragon. Bea puts it in everything," The blonde stated as if it were actually why she was there. It was then that Harper saw who had been talking, at which moment, she went pale.

Judith looked from one to the other. Without another word, she walked out of the kitchen. Whether she believed the explanation or not, she was gone.

"That's—" Harper's eyes were wide as Buzz slammed a hand over Harper's mouth. The sisters just looked into each other's eyes until Harper nodded at the redhead. They had some communication that he couldn't understand.

"I'll see you later," Buzz stated, letting her go.

"You will. I'll be at the house at exactly 9 p.m."

"Be alone," Buzz replied and pushed her out the door, slamming it behind her.

Buzz turned and straightened her coat as she came towards him. "I have work to do, Jonas."

He raised an eyebrow. "What was that about?"

"Nothing, just a sister thing." She checked the French toasts and started flipping them.

"Does she know who Judith is?" he asked her in confusion.

"No, she just looks like someone we know. But it's not her. Now go eat breakfast." She dismissed him.

Ignoring her, he leaned against the counter, close enough to her that her coat brushed his bare arm. "Maybe I want to make out with the chef this morning."

It was exactly what he wanted to do. It was the same thing he wanted every morning.

"She has no time today," Buzz replied sharply.

He pushed off the counter, sensing she wasn't in a good mood anymore. "I have meetings all day today, so you don't have to make chicken salad for me."

"Good, I'm running low on it," she said and then cringed. She had just been caught serving the same meal until it ran out.

He smiled at her reaction. "How many days are you serving it?"

"Until Judith eats here once. Then I'll change the menu," she admitted.

"At least you're honest." He kissed her forehead, which made her wince before leaving her to do her work.

Heading up the stairs, he met Louisa coming down. He had expected her to look like death warmed over, but she looked just like every other day.

"Morning, Louisa."

"Jonas." Her tone wasn't nearly as loving as it was the night before.

"How are you feeling?"

"Good. Better than expected," she said and smiled at him with her backpack over her shoulder. Maybe she wasn't going to skip school that day, which meant she felt a lot better than she had the day before. Maybe the night out was what she needed.

CHAPTER EIGHTEEN

After dreading 9 p.m. all day, she was surprised when Harper wasn't there when she got home. Nor was Agatha; hopefully, her sister was living her best life while Sera was gone because Buzz was spending her time falling for her stepbrother, and that was a big mistake.

Today she had strengthened her resolve to stay away from the man, which was easy when he was busy and out of the house. It was much harder when he was dragging her to his bedroom for sex—hot, dirty sex because it was the only kind he knew. And now it was the only kind she liked.

Since she didn't get a chance to move her stuff from Maby's bedroom the night before, she took some time to get her stuff organized. Not that either room was better than the other, but she had always liked Harper's room better since it had two windows.

With the bed cleared off, she went to the bathroom and changed into her "Buzzzz" pajama's and washed her face. Drinking and sex all night made her tired. Back in her room, there was a key in the middle of her new bed.

Grabbing them, she went to Harper's room and found her sitting cross-legged on her bed. She was in leggings and her favorite yellow

"Yellin Stan" T-shirt. When she saw Buzz, she tapped her bed for her to sit down also, which was probably a trap. Harper liked to lure her prey to her.

"How did you know it was her?" Buzz asked. It had been years since any of the sisters had seen their mother.

"I looked her up a few years ago. Though 'Raiden' didn't make it click, her face did. The few articles I found had pictures of her and her husband. How did you find her?"

"I was in line to talk to Chelsea about Mom's house, and she was in front of me. She's using her maiden name, Rowley. I followed her and got her to hire me as a chef. I had to see if it was really her or not."

"So, no story?" Harper asked.

"I could interview Jonas, but I think that ship has sailed. He would never give me an interview, and really, why would he? I'm a nobody, and I don't even work for a paper anymore. I got fired."

"It's about time, Buzzy. You can do so much better than the Times," Harper stated as usual.

"I like being a reporter," Buzz argued.

"No, you didn't. You played the part well, though. I'll talk to Bex about getting you a job at Hawthorn; publicity is where you need to be. And since you have experience in reporting, I think she would like someone with your knowledge." Harper stated, about the Director of Marketing at her husband's company, who just happened to also be her sister-in-law.

"I don't need anyone to hand me a job. I happen to have a job." Buzz said, then remembered she didn't have a job. Not a real one anyway.

"You're pretending to be a chef for our mother. How long is that going to last?"

"Not long. I was just staying until I knew for sure she was the right Judith. Now I know, so I can quit. I don't even remember her. Was she really always just bitchy?"

"From what I remember, she wasn't that fond of children. The noise was what she complained about all the time. Headaches, noise, and needing to be alone. I was in charge of keeping the four of you quiet, and I wasn't very good at it."

"I can't see any of us girls being silent for more than a minute. Maybe Maby, when she's reading. Lucy, though? Never." Harper shook her head

"I don't think I'm going to tell her who I am. At this point, I don't even like her." Buzz hated to say it out loud, but it was true.

Harper only nodded. "What about the brother? Or the sister for that matter? Wait, is Louisa hers?"

Buzz smirked. "You mean Louisa May Alcott Raiden? I don't know for sure."

Harper rolled her eyes. "Another sister? I knew I liked her right away, but actually having another sister is going to be weird. And she's so different from the rest of us."

"She's nineteen—a lot younger than us. Oh, and I'm sleeping with her brother. Kind of gross, but god, I love him!" After the words were out of her mouth, she stopped and corrected herself. "It. *It* is what I love, not him."

Harper let the admission slide. "Are you going to tell him? You can't really have a relationship with him if he doesn't know his step-mother is your mom."

"Sera's my mother; I didn't even remember Judith. She left us without a care and never looked back. There's no place in my life for her," Buzz said, and it was true. Judith would never have a place in her life, and after all this time, she probably wouldn't want one.

"At this point, I think we have to tell Louisa. She deserves to know she has a big family here to fall back on, no matter what happens in life," Harper stated, being a big sister even to the newest member.

"Judith chose to raise her. Even now, she loves to have her nearby. What makes her special?" Their mother choosing a favorite was hard for Buzz, even at twenty-five.

"That's something we'll probably never know." Harper shrugged. "But if you are falling for Jonas, and she is a part of his life, you share a sister."

"I am *not* falling for him," Buzz argued, pulling her knees under her.

"Okay, Buzzy, believe your little lies, but I was right where you are not that long ago." Harper patted her shoulder. It was oddly comforting, coming from a woman who would just as soon punch you than hug you.

Groaning, Buzz stated, "You were sleeping with your boss."

"I was, but I was also falling for someone I shouldn't have. I really tried not to, and what I learned is that no matter how hard you fight it, you can't control your heart." Harper pressed a hand to her heart with a smile.

"I'm better at this than you are, Harper."

"Keep telling yourself that, but I have to get home. Kaine doesn't want me to stay out all night."

"Thanks for stopping by and talking."

"You can have my room. I'm sorry I said you couldn't have it. It's just sometimes it's nice to know I have a place if I need to get away from Kaine. But I don't want to be away from him, ever, so you can have the room."

"I am still taking Mom's when she finally moves out. I need a bathroom."

"You'll only have to share with Agatha if Lucy takes the master, so maybe it's not as big of a deal as when we were all here."

"I haven't seen Agatha all week. Granted, I'm not here all the time, but I feel she hasn't been here either."

"Good for her." Harper grinned and fist-pumped the air. They were both on the same wavelength that their sister needed a few days of away time. "I think the wedding took a lot out of her." She and Sera had always been close, and now that Sera has Harrison, he displaced their little sister. "Call me if she isn't back by the weekend, and I'll start texting her to see if she's okay."

"I did yesterday, and she said she was fine." She shrugged, not believing it so much as the first time she had gotten the text.

"Then I won't worry too much. Call if you need anything." Harper held up her phone, as if Buzz needed to know what to use to call.

"I will. Do you know when Lucy's coming home?" Buzz asked before realizing she shouldn't have asked Harper. She wouldn't know.

"I don't know. She stopped talking to me for some reason … probably that fancy job Mom got her," Harper mumbled as she left the room.

Listening to her go down the steps and out the door, Buzz felt the house closing in on her. Once again, she was here alone. It was silent, and every little noise was starting to freak her out. Grabbing her phone, she turned on Harper's clock radio to a local station and left the room, doing the same in Mabel's room before she headed down the stairs. With all the lights off, she curled up on the couch and turned the TV on. She still felt alone, but at least there was noise back in the big house.

CHAPTER NINETEEN

Friday morning came early for Jonas with a call from half-way around the world. Harrison called him from his honeymoon to tell him that Raiden & Son's Financial had been raided at 2 a.m. and to not to go into the office. The closer the raid got, the more on edge he was about it, so he had been avoiding work more and more.

By 6 a.m., he watched Buzz's Jeep park in her usual place and jumped to help her bring in the breakfast that he was almost one-hundred-percent sure she didn't make. In fact, he was sure her vehicle was riddled with receipts for the breakfasts she hadn't been making all week. How she was getting supper, he had no idea, and so far, she hadn't dazzled Judith with her chicken salad, so she didn't have to change out that menu item.

"Jonas, you're up early," she said as she opened the back door and grabbed out the six containers of food.

"Just waiting for my favorite chef to show up." He took the containers from her, wishing he could instead pin her to her car and make her whimper. He loved when she whimpered.

"I hope she shows up soon." Buzz only half-joked as she followed him into the house.

They made quick work of setting out the food. Then he was able to pin her to the wall of the kitchen and make her make noises he'd dreamed about hearing. The woman had gotten under his skin. He couldn't think when she was around, but he couldn't think when she was gone either. He barely knew her but trusted her completely.

After successfully getting her jacket off, she pushed him away before he could take off her shirt, leaving her breasts secure in the pink shirt that had a "D" on it, except it was sideways, making it just look like a smiling mouth.

"I have to work, Jonas. Besides, this is not happening today." Her words were said with such conviction, just like every morning since after she got drunk with Louisa. He almost believed her.

"I don't care. Take today off and spend the day in my room—alone and naked," he whispered in her ear.

The shiver that ran through her body said she was very much into the idea, but her mind was still pushing him away. "No, no. I'm a professional."

"But a professional what?" He had her trapped between his arms and pinned to the wall still.

"Jonas Arthur Raiden, get your hands off that woman!" Judith's voice was nearly shrill as she said the words.

Springing back from Buzz, he turned and glared at the woman. Who was she to say whom he could and could not talk to? Or anything else for that matter.

"This does not concern you, Judith," Jonas stated, his anger palpable.

"Really? She is my employee, and you are a guest in this house. Whatever this is must stop."

"Jonas, she's right," Buzz said from behind him. "I'll just get my stuff together and leave."

Grabbing her arm, he stopped her. "She's going nowhere, Judith."

"I am her boss, Jonas, not you. Now she's fired because I warned her more than once about this kind of activity. She knew better than to seduce you, but then again, you always have been very seducible. Besides, isn't twenty-five a bit young for you?"

"How do you know how old I am?" Buzz demanded suddenly.

Judith stopped moving and opened her mouth only to close it again, then stated with a smug grin, "Your application."

Buzz stopped talking for a moment and stared at Judith before calmly replying, "I lied on my application, which means you know who I am. After all these years, you still don't care about me. I think I'll just finish out the day, seeing as how I'm already here and would like a full week on my paycheck."

"I think not." She huffed.

"Then I'll have to talk to George about some things. We have a lot to talk about, don't we?" Buzz asked Judith, who was suddenly very pale.

Judith waved off the redhead before leaving the kitchen. "Do what you must, but you're finished here. And Jonas, leave her alone. We don't need her kind here."

"My kind, as if you know anything about me. Anything at all!" Buzz yelled after her, suddenly angry. Her face was red with it.

"Buzz, stop. I am so sorry about her. I would be willing to give you a recommendation anytime or anywhere. You're an amazing chef, and really, this job wasn't all that great." He tried to calm her, make her see that being fired was for the best.

"It's not that; jobs are jobs," she mumbled and pushed out of his arms. "I have to get water for your dad and Louisa."

"I'll hire you, Buzz—I'm serious. I have a house and hate to cook. You can …" he started.

"No, just leave it. I knew wouldn't last. I guess I thought I would be the one to quit first, but I didn't think she knew," Buzz said, but she wasn't exactly talking to him.

"Knew what?"

Buzz took a breath and said, "Nothing, just forget it. Us, you and me, that wasn't going to last anyway. There's just too much there for anything to be possible."

"What are you talking about?"

"Nothing, just go. You have to go to work or something, right?" She waved him off.

"No, not today. I've been waiting an entire month for today." He took a step closer to her, not letting her push him away.

"Do you want to talk about it?" she asked in surprise.

"Yes, actually, I do. I would love to tell someone about it, anyone," he admitted. After only talking to Harrison and the feds, he would love to tell someone else, someone who didn't care about the outcome and would just be on his side.

Instead of asking more, Buzz took a step away from him. "I ... I can't talk about it with you. Please, I'm sorry I even asked."

Her face was pale as she said it; her entire body was stiff.

"Jonas, there's a woman who wants to talk to you," Louisa stated from the door, her eyes on both of them.

"I'll be right there, Louisa." Jonas waved her off before turning back to Buzz. "I want to talk to you. About us."

Buzz's nod was barely noticeable as she stared at him. He reluctantly left her in the kitchen as he headed out to the door to see who wanted to talk to him. He was expecting a federal agent or a lawyer from Harrison's office since Harrison was still in Hawaii. Instead, it was a blonde woman in a tight skirt and black jacket.

"Jonas Raiden? I'm Meghan Murphy from the Times. I was hoping you would have time for an interview this morning," the woman stated with a perfect smile.

"Get out of my house," he replied angrily. Harrison had warned him that the reporters would find him quickly.

"Just a few questions; my readers want to hear your side of the story. Your uncle says he was framed."

"Out of the house." He pointed at the door, knowing he couldn't physically remove her.

"My readers are interested in your side of all this. When did you start thinking your uncle had been stealing from the company? How long has it been happening?" her questions came quickly.

"No comment. Now get out," he repeated.

The reporter's smile faltered as she looked beyond him. Turning slightly, he saw Buzz and Louisa coming down the hallway from the kitchen, most likely drawn by the noise and commotion. The reporter's frown flashed with anger. "What is she doing here? No wonder you won't talk to me."

"Excuse me?" he demanded, not knowing if she was talking about his sister or the chef.

Ignoring Jonas's question, she looked at Buzz and said, "What are you doing here? Wait, are you undercover? You are, aren't you?"

"I was fired; you know that," Buzz stated and crossed her arms over her still open jacket. It was obvious that they knew each other.

"Fired my ass. You were planted in this house for the story. Have you gotten it?" Meghan demanded, then gave a shy smile at the chef.

"I'm not working on a story," Buzz hissed at her.

"Bea Bradford always looks for the story, isn't that right, Bea? Wow, undercover." The woman seemed impressed.

"What's going on?" Jonas demanded.

"I guess I'll leave since he isn't talking to me anyway. But he is talking to you, isn't he?" Meghan stated and turned to leave finally.

"What is she talking about?" he demanded. His confusion was starting to clear up.

"She has no idea what she's talking about."

"Are you a reporter?" he demanded, his anger palpable.

Buzz blinked once and then admitted, "I was, but not anymore. I can't catch a break."

"So, you decided to come here undercover? Can you even cook? You can't, can you?" He knew she couldn't. Not once had she even pretended to cook a meal in the kitchen. Everything was prepackaged, or she'd bought it on the way over, yet he had never questioned it —until now.

"Uhm, I-I can explain," she stammered.

"Go ahead. Explain why you're pretending to be a chef when you can't even cook. It isn't to get a story?" he demanded loudly.

Buzz looked at him, then at Louisa and back to him, "It wasn't for a story." Her voice was quiet as she said it.

"Not for a story? Then why? What reason did you have to pretend to be a chef?"

"It's not about you. I didn't even know you were here," she

reminded him. She had been just as surprised as he was when they had met in the kitchen that day.

"How did you know there was even a story here? Long enough ago to lie on your resume to get a job here a week ago, apparently. Only a handful of people knew. How did you know?" he asked. When she was in his closet, she'd been a reporter—an unethical one.

She backed away from him. "I have to leave."

"No way, lady. Tell me how you know. Wait, what were you doing in that closet? Was that for a story? Was everything for a story?" He needed her to say it. Or, more importantly, to explain that it wasn't for a story and that it had all been a mistake. There had to be an explanation for it, any explanation.

Straightening her back, she answered, "Yes. I mean, no. I was trying to get a story, but I failed. And got fired for it."

She had admitted that she had only wanted a story. All of this had been for a story. He had fallen for her, but she was there for a story and nothing more. He had been a fool.

CHAPTER TWENTY

"YOU SLEPT with me just to get a story for the paper?" Jonas barked at her in anger.

Buzz flinched at the words. She knew they weren't true, but no matter how she looked at it, they sounded true. How could she tell him that the moment he walked into that hotel room, she'd decided that she couldn't write about him anymore? That she couldn't do that to him? He wouldn't believe her.

"No," she tried and stopped. He wasn't listening; he was too angry at her.

Louisa took a step away from her; her expression conveying that she believed what Jonas was saying. But Buzz couldn't tell him she was there to see Judith, that she had to know if the woman was her mother or not. She didn't want Louisa to find out the truth like this. Just a few days before, Buzz had been shocked at learning she had another sister, but Louisa was going to find out about five.

"I hope you don't think you can publish the story. I will sue your paper so fast that you won't even remember your name if that happens," Jonas threatened.

"I wouldn't. You know me; I wouldn't do something like that," she argued. He had to realize he knew her better than Meghan Murphy did.

"I don't know anything about you, Miss Bradford. I never have." He walked past her and then up the stairs, leaving her and Louisa alone in the entryway.

"Are you really a reporter?" Louisa asked.

"I was. Not a good one, but I was," she admitted after hearing Jonas slam a door on the floor above them.

"I think you should leave my family alone then." Louisa took another step away from her.

She and Louisa had rushed to the front of the house when they'd heard the commotion, but the look in the younger woman's eyes said that they were not friends anymore.

Without a word, she turned and walked down the hallway, away from her younger sister, who would never know she had a family out there that would love to have her in it. But she wouldn't leave this family for the Lovelys; Buzz knew that. No matter how dysfunctional this one was, it was still her family.

As she walked through the kitchen, she left everything she had there, which was a few T-shirts, in case she spilled, and a few pans of leftovers in the fridge. There was nothing worth stopping for.

How had everything gotten so messed up in less than an hour? Judith had all but admitted she was her mother and that she didn't want anything to do with Buzz or any of her sisters, except Louisa. By admitting she knew how old Buzz was, she was also admitting she knew who Buzz was, but she wasn't willing to tell anyone else, which meant that nobody else knew about her or any of her sisters.

And now Jonas hated her and would forever hate her, thinking that she betrayed him. All because she had to see if Judith was her mother, which had been a mistake because today, just like last month, her mother didn't want anything to do with her. It still hurt that she kind of wanted her mom to care a little for her.

In two days, Sera would be back, and Buzz knew she loved her and cared about what happened to her. And most days, it was all she needed, but today, she had wanted Judith to say something. *Anything.*

The drive home was a blur, as was unloading the cooler back into the freezer. No need to thaw the meals she didn't need anymore. She knew she would quit one day, but she'd wanted to do it on the day she had chosen.

Up in Harper's room, she stared out the window at the tree in the neighbor's back yard. It was the same view she always saw from Harper's bed. Today she got lost in just staring at it. Hours later, she was still staring at the tree as darkness settled out her window. Her phone had buzzed with a few texts and messages until she knew it died; she'd forgotten to charge it. Not that it mattered; nobody was calling or texting her anymore.

When her bladder threatened to burst, she got up and checked on Agatha. From the stairway, she saw her lying in her own bed in the early evening, a time when her sister was usually getting up. Buzz knew she had made noise on the way up, but her sister didn't move.

Buzz slowly walked up the steps in hopes that her sister would want to talk. Agatha was always the one with all the answers. Though she had no life of her own, she was pretty good at straightening out everyone else's attempts at it.

When her sister still didn't move, Buzz kicked off her shoes and let Harper's chef's jacket fall to the floor as she walked to the bed. Her sister didn't make a sound as she went.

Crawling into bed with her, she wrapped her arms around Agatha. It had been years since Buzz had needed comfort from her sister, but tonight, she felt they both could use it. No matter what Agatha had been up to, she hadn't had sex in a pantry with their stepbrother. She hadn't lied about being a chef to find out information on their mother, only to have Jonas think it was about him. That was all Buzz.

"I messed up this week. So badly," Buzz admitted in the dark, her voice thick with the tears she had been fighting for hours now.

"Me too." Agatha's voice was just as thick as she let Buzz hold her, and they let their mistakes be forgiven.

They didn't say anything else, just held on to each other all night, neither admitting that they or their sister was crying in the darkness.

But Buzz was happy she wasn't alone when she had done so many bad things in her life, or just in the last few days.

CHAPTER TWENTY-ONE

Harrison was back in the state and on his way over. For three days, Jonas had stayed at his father's house. For nearly all of them, he hadn't talked to anyone except Harrison. Jonas was hiding from reporters. Or just one.

Even if the lawyer had left seven messages on his phone before announcing he was just coming over, Jonas still wasn't actually ready to talk to anyone. After some not-so-pleasant greetings, Harrison stated, "I talked to Agent Conley. Since Harvey had the foresight to talk to a reporter and make you look like you were involved, we're going to do an interview ourselves. It's the only way."

"If you think it will help," Jonas replied, but he was done with reporters. After sleeping with one for over a week, he never wanted to see another reporter again.

"I think it will help get your side to the public. And since there's no information pointing at you, there is no way you're going to be in any trouble. This would just get you some good PR, which is something your company will be needing a lot of when this is settled."

"I still worry."

"That's why we're doing the interview. I know the perfect reporter.

So far, she hasn't gotten many big interviews, but I think she'd be up for it."

"As long as it's not Meghan Murphy from the Times, I'm up for anyone." Well, not anyone, but there was no way Harrison would find the one reporter Jonas wanted nothing to do with.

"Her name is Bea Bradford, and she's perfect," he stated louder than anything else he had said. "Sorry, Sera made me say that."

"Fuck no. Not that bitch," Jonas hissed. In what universe did her name come out of his friend's mouth? "Do you know her?"

Is that how she knew what he was doing? How she knew last week about the entire thing? She had been in the closet after two days after he started talking to the feds.

"I can find someone else if you don't want her." Harrison dodged the question, but that was answer enough for Jonas.

"Anyone else," he mumbled and sat up in bed, hating that he would now need to shower and probably shave after a week of doing neither.

"I'll call you when I know who the reporter will be. For now, just stick to your dad's house and don't talk to anyone."

"Don't worry. I have no one to talk to." He hung up on the man and tossed his phone on the bed. He still saw his naked redhead in it, even if she had only spent one night there.

Flopping down on the same bed, he covered his eyes with his hands. This was even worse than he had thought it would be. He loved his uncle and didn't want him in prison, but he was a thief and con man; he couldn't just walk free.

"How are you?" Louisa asked from the doorway. Glancing up at her for a moment, she reminded him of Buzz in the blue T-shirt and tight jeans, just like she would have worn.

"Fine, I guess."

"Dad told me about Uncle Harvey. Is he really going to jail?"

"Probably. Shouldn't you be in school today?" He wondered what day it was but was sure it was a weekday.

"No, I just can't. Not after your fight with Buzz. There's just so much going on around here," Louisa replied, but Jonas wondered if it was more that she wasn't interested in her classes when the house was so active.

"Sorry you had to see that."

"I don't think she's writing a story about you. She never asked me questions about you at all. If she was writing a story about you, she would have asked a ton of them," Louisa explained as she walked into the room.

"Reporters are sneaky."

"Buzz wasn't. She was always nice to me, even if Mom didn't want her to be. The night I went out with her and Harper, they were both nice to me. They didn't have to be."

"Where did you go that night?"

"Some bar by her house. It was so much fun; I wish I had friends like them. Real friends. I tried to call her all weekend, but her phone is off," Louisa said as if telling him she had already forgiven Buzz. But Jonas wasn't quite ready yet.

"Don't call her, Louisa. Just let it go. Make different friends," he suggested.

"I looked up some of her articles on the internet. She didn't get any pieces close to an interview with you. Mostly just weddings and such. Maybe she tried to interview you but then couldn't. She said she got fired, so I called the paper to check. She no longer works there." Louisa leaned against his dresser, smiling.

"What was she doing here then? Why was she here?"

"I don't know. Maybe you could ask her," Louisa suggested.

"I did, but she didn't say."

"Just try and forgive her. You liked her and you were pretty happy when she was around."

"It was just sex."

"I'm young, Jonas, but not stupid." She tapped his leg and left the room, leaving him alone with his thoughts.

Closing his eyes, he tried not to picture her unable to talk, to explain what she had been doing there.

A scream snapped him out of his mind and had him running to his sister—there was nobody else in the house that had that scream. He found her in the hallway, staring into the room Brett and Ross were sharing. Louisa's face was completely white.

George had come running from the other direction and was now looking in the room as well. All eyes were glued to the scene before them: Judith was sandwiched between the two young men, and all three were almost completely naked. As much as he wanted to, it wasn't a sight that Jonas was ever going to forget.

Judith's face was pale as she was caught by her husband, stepson, and daughter in the middle of a threesome with two men well under half her age. Jonas grabbed Louisa and pulled her away from the door and back towards his room, which was across from her own.

Pushing her into her room, he told her to stay, noticing that her face was pale, and her eyes were huge. The shock he was feeling was even worse for his sister. She had the hots for one of those men in the room that her mother was screwing.

Down the hallway, he could hear his father's voice. Maybe this time, the divorce would take. George seeing what his wife was up to was maybe what the older man needed.

"Is this why you wanted him here? Because he was your lover?!" George bellowed.

"I can explain," Judith argued as she was pulling on her clothes, the boys behind her doing the same.

George turned his back on her and continued, "Explain to my lawyer, Judith. You two young men will be leaving as soon as you get clothes on. And you also, Judith. And don't bother taking Louisa; she's staying with me."

"You can't keep my daughter from me!" Judith argued, but there was no strength in her words. This time, she had done something unforgiving in George's eyes, and she knew it.

"I can and I will. If she wants to contact you, that is up to her, but she will not be living with you. You can go back to Chicago and keep the house. I'm already giving you enough money to live on, but this is over," George stated.

"George, really?" Judith begged.

"Get out of my house," George hissed.

Judith stepped out of the room and into the hallway, completely dressed again, which was the only thing that made Jonas happy. "Louisa, pack a bag. We're leaving," she said, ignoring her husband's words.

George turned to her, yelling, "I said no! She will stay here."

Judith glared at George and replied, "Fine, I didn't want her anyway. You were the one who always wanted her. I was tired of kids, but you wanted to have another. Well, now you have her."

"Yes, I do." George didn't seem bothered by what the woman had said about her own daughter.

Behind him, he heard a gasp; Louisa had heard it all. Her hand was covering her mouth, and there were giant tears in her eyes, which made her look seven again.

"Louisa." Jonas reached for her to give her a hug, but she side-stepped and ran past him into the hallway.

Her parents saw her, but neither moved as she rushed past them towards the stairs, then down them until she was gone. Growling at the couple, he rushed after her. Neither of them saw that the kid was falling apart or that their words had hurt her so badly.

Jonas searched outside, but he couldn't find her. Back inside, he searched the house, then went back outside and looked again. Ross and Brett both left with their suitcases within minutes. Judith took closer to an hour, but she was quick to leave as well. Louisa had left with nothing and hadn't returned yet when the sun had set.

The only way he stopped worrying was when she sent him a text that she was okay, just two letters that didn't seem like enough.

CHAPTER TWENTY-TWO

"YOUR MOTHER DID *WHAT?*" Buzz asked, trying to hear Louisa above the cacophony of all her sisters talking at once in the kitchen.

Stepping away from the non-stop noise, she headed into the living room. Today the sisters had gathered on the day Sera and Harrison were coming home with the kids, and as a surprise, they were going to move as much of Sera's stuff into the new house as possible, thus forcing Sera to actually move in with her husband.

"She was having sex with Brett and Ross at the same time," Louisa repeated with the same monotone she had used the first time she had said it; Buzz hadn't heard wrong. She still couldn't believe it, but she hadn't heard wrong.

"Wow," was all she could think to say. Judith seemed to be so conservative and against sex in general.

"Can you come and get me? I can't stay here." Louisa sniffled into the phone.

"Yes, give me ten, and I'll be there," Buzz said as Harper looked in the living room at her.

"Thanks. I'm not at the house, so call me when you get close." Louisa hung up.

After slipping her phone into her pocket, she told her sister, "I'm going to get Louisa."

"Is that wise?" Harper asked.

"Maybe, I don't know, but Judith was just caught fucking the kid Louisa liked, so I can't *not* go get her. No matter what happened between me and her brother." Buzz sighed.

Harper gave a concerned look before telling her. "Tell her I told her guys were shit."

Buzz nodded and headed out the door to bring one more sister back to the fold. The drive was short, and Louisa was waiting a block from her house with nothing on but a light sweatshirt and jeans. She was shivering in the chilly afternoon sun. The winter weather was too cold for the outfit, and Buzz was mad once again at Judith for letting her daughter leave without a jacket on, though it sounded like the woman had been busy when she left.

Louisa climbed into the Jeep and said nothing to Buzz as they headed back to the house. As they approached, she saw nothing but an ant trail of people carrying boxes the two blocks from the old house to the new house. Never was Buzz so glad that two of her sisters had husbands to help with this endeavor. It was a cold day, but the trip was short, and the chill made everyone move faster.

"We're moving my stepmom out of the house. It's a surprise for her wedding," Buzz explained.

"Wouldn't she want to move her own stuff?" Louisa watched as Cliff carried a giggling Maby back into the Lovely house over his shoulder.

"No, she likes us too much to actually move herself. We're kicking her out."

"My mom doesn't want me anymore … she never did. She didn't even care that I heard her say it." The kid shrugged, and her voice cracked.

"Mom's suck. My real mom didn't want me either, or any of my sisters. Sera's our stepmom," she admitted, though she probably shouldn't have.

"I didn't know that."

"You'll figure it out once she gets here; she's very different from the rest of us. But now, let me introduce you to everyone who is here." Buzz jumped out of the car.

At the door, they nearly got run over by Kaine carrying more than he could see around. The man was already tired of this and had offered more than once to pay someone to actually do the moving, but nobody else seemed interested in wasting money. It was much more fun to see him scowl and have to work.

"Kaine is married to Harper." Buzz pointed at him. Then in the house, she pointed to Lucy and Maby, who were sitting on the couch. "The twins; don't tell them they look alike," she whispered.

"One is my children's lit professor, or at least I think so. I only went to one class," Louisa stated, as if she ran into professors every day in their homes, arguing with their identical twin.

Then she introduced Louisa to Cliff and finally Agatha, who was shoving Emma's things in boxes so fast the room was nearly empty already. Taking the girl to Harper's room, she found a sweatshirt for her to wear and informed her she really didn't have to help. But after all the teasing she had already witnessed, she said she would have more fun helping than moping around.

Harper only gave her a nod and insisted that everyone call the girl Lou, which everyone did after an hour. No one questioned who she was, not even Maby, who was her teacher.

Within an hour, the moving was interrupted by the bride and groom's arrival at Lovely house. Sera caught Harper and Maby holding Lucy down, trying to make her eat something that had been found in Violet's room.

That prompted Sera to immediately tell her new husband, "This is why I cannot move out. They'll kill each other!"

The sisters let their captive go so that everyone could hug the travelers. Harper was the first to tell the older woman, "Mom, we are kicking you out."

"What did I do?" Sera was already on the verge of tears.

"You got married, so you've got to move out. Those are the rules," Agatha stated from her spot on the couch. Despite the heat of the house and work, she was snuggled under a blanket.

"I knew I shouldn't have gotten married," Sera grumbled and looked around the room at the scattered boxes. Clearly, the movers had gotten distracted as the day went on.

"Don't worry, Sera. We kicked Mabel and Harper out the exact same way," Buzz said as she handed out drinks she had grabbed from the kitchen. "Finally!"

"No, you didn't. They both still have rooms here," Lucy argued, getting up off the floor.

"I gave mine to Buzz a few days ago," Harper stated, though unlocking it had just seemed like a nice gesture, not an "I'm giving up my room" gesture. Buzz was sure that if she needed it, Harper would happily kick her sister out again.

"I told Maby she could have a room here if I got one at her place. It only seemed fair," Lucy argued for her twin, the moldy cupcake forgotten.

"I don't believe any of it," Sera announced and threw up her hands.

"I just want to thank everyone for helping Sera through this challenging time in her life. Moving a block and a half from you girls is hard for her. I don't know if anyone even noticed that." Harrison pulled his wife into his arms as he made his speech.

"Yeah, she was hiding that from everyone." Buzz snorted at them.

"I'm very good at hiding things from you people, Buzz," Sera stated, then broke down laughing at what she said.

"What are you hiding, Sera?" Harper grinned and eyed her critically.

"Nothing. But I could if I wanted to," Sera reminded them. "Now move these boxes out. I want to be completely moved in by nightfall."

"So that you can have sex with your husband in your house with all your stuff?" Agatha asked.

"For your information, yes," Sera shot back at her.

"Gross, Mom. I'm right here." Emma dropped her bag and headed up the stairway away from everyone.

"Love you too, baby," Sera called after her, which only was rewarded by her baby giving her the finger. "I think I have to learn to control my language."

"The first step is admitting it, Mom," Maby stated with a grin.

Above them, a door slammed, and Emma came back down the steps. "Where's all my shit?"

"In your new room down the street," Lucy replied cheerfully.

"I'm not leaving! I'm staying here. Just because she moves out doesn't mean I have to."

"Nope, you get to move in with your mommy and daddy," Buzz told her. That had always been the plan. No way was Sera letting one of her actual babies not live with her until the law said they could pry themselves from her. Even then, it was going to be a hard fight.

"I think I'm old enough to live here. This is my home." Emma crossed her arms.

"Me too." Violet had maneuvered herself under Agatha's blanket and was sitting on her lap.

"No, no, no. Both my children are moving with me, and anyone else for that matter. Don't let Harrison tell you that you're not welcome, and we have room for everyone," Sera assured everyone.

"Not everyone," Harrison argued.

"Almost everyone. A few might have to sleep on the couches. And no husbands; that would be too many."

"So, if you're married, you're not welcome?" Maby asked.

"Maby, you are always welcome. I know which room I'd put you in already. Just no Cliff." Sera pulled away from Harrison and gave Maby a tight hug.

"Harsh, Mom Lovely," Cliff stated from the doorway of the kitchen, where the men were hiding from the moving boxes. Sera gave him the finger as she continued to hug his wife.

"Why does she get a room? She already has two," Harper pointed out.

Letting go of Maby, she pulled Harper in for a hug as well. "You have a room too."

"Do I get a room, Mom?" Agatha asked from the couch.

"Of course. Next to Violet's. She'll like that."

Lucy realized everyone was getting something and needed it also. "Wait, I want to room."

"You can share with Maby again. The twins will be back in the same room, except no boys this time." Sera hugged the other twin as she said it.

"I get the house! You can move over there if you want, which will leave me here, and the house can be mine." Buzz laughed. Even though she hated it empty, she really liked to win.

"If she's staying, so am I." Agatha changed sides.

"Me too. Even if I haven't been here this week, I still live here," Lucy jumped in quickly.

"Can I have a room?" Louisa asked from the corner where she'd been watching.

All eyes turned to her, especially those that didn't know who she was. Sera walked over to her slowly, looking her up and down. In the red sweatshirt, she looked more like Harper than Buzz remembered, just younger and more innocent than Harper ever looked.

"And you are?"

"Louisa Raiden, ma'am. I am a friend of Buzz's."

Sera looked back at Buzz with a questioning look, then turned back to the girl and gave her as big of a hug as she had given all her kids. "Of course, Louisa. This is the Lovely house. Everyone is welcome here."

"Thank you, ma'am." Buzz could hear the tears in the girl's voice. Once again, Sera was a mother to a girl she didn't have to be, just like she had been to all of them over the years.

"But if you ever call me ma'am again, you're out. It's Sera Dean." Sera actually hugged Louisa again in her excitement of being married.

"Thank you, Sera."

Buzz was nearly in tears as she watched. She wondered if Sera could tell Louisa was a sister, that she had another lost soul to save. Only this time, Louisa wasn't a child, and she knew who her parents were and had been with them her entire life. So different from the rest of them.

Catching Harper's eyes across the room, she saw the same look in her eyes.

CHAPTER TWENTY-THREE

T H E   H O U S E   H A D   B E E N   D E A F E N I N G L Y quiet for the last few days as Jonas let the dust settle. Since his arrest, Harvey had denied everything. From a jail cell, he had been pointing the finger at Jonas, as if he hadn't been like a son to the man for a decade.

As much as Jonas hated the idea of an interview, he was starting to see that it was the only way to clear his name. Harvey was talking to everyone and anyone and lying the entire time. Jonas had to fight him as much as he could in the papers as well it seemed.

Harrison had set up an interview with a woman named Grace Atwater. Jonas had never heard of her, but since he said no to Bea and Meghan, he was left with her. Though after a day of thinking about it, he knew he should have just given the interview to Bea Bradford since she had worked so hard to get an interview from him in the first place. But then again, he hated to reward her for her actions.

"I've read some of Atwater's stories, and I think she'll do great with this kind of article. Have you had a chance to look over the articles I sent you?" Harrison asked as they walked into the paper's office.

"No, I trust you," he said. He hadn't been doing anything over the last few days except thinking about Buzz and everything that had happened between them in the time he knew her. From the night in the hotel until she admitted she had been doing everything for a story. Everything.

Louisa hadn't returned to the house since her mom and the boys left. He had texted her that Judith was gone, but still, the girl didn't come home. She was staying with friends, was all she said. No address or any more information about where she was.

"I couldn't have gotten you Bea Bradford even if you'd wanted her. She got fired." Harrison led him through the busy entry of the newspaper.

"Did you talk to her about me?" he asked. It was the only link he could think of for her to know what was going on before it actually happened.

"No, especially not her since she's a reporter—*was* a reporter. I haven't heard what she plans to do now," Harrison stated.

"I'm sure that getting out of reporting isn't actually going to happen for her," Jonas argued. He knew the woman better than Harrison did, after all.

"Do you know her?" Harrison stopped and looked at him.

"She spent some time stalking me. I finally figured her out, though. Sent her packing," he finally admitted.

"Why didn't you tell me? I could have talked to her about it."

"I didn't realize it for a few days."

"You didn't notice a Lovely for days? She must be losing her touch." Harrison chuckled as he opened the door to a conference room with a lone woman at the table. For a second, he had hoped it would be Buzz. Instead, the woman was a stranger, and he didn't want to talk to her at all.

"Jonas Raiden? I'm Grace Atwater. Nice to meet you." The woman stood up with a wide smile on her face.

"Nice to meet you as well, Grace," he said.

"Mr. Dean, thank you for bringing him in." Grace sat down and looked at her paper.

An hour later, the interview was over, and Grace seemed happy with what he had told her. More than pleased with her questions, it seemed.

"Thank you for the interview, Jonas. I will send the perliminary article to Harrison for approval before we run it. I can almost guarantee the front page with this."

"Thank you, Grace, for doing this for me."

"I'm just happy you didn't go with Meghan, but after she almost broke into your house, I can understand it. I had assumed Bea would get the article, but her loss is my gain. Leave it to her to land in the middle of a front-page article and mess it up. That's Bea." Grace chuckled to herself.

"Maybe she was just never given a chance around here," Harrison stated as he pushed Jonas out of the door. Jonas could hear an edge to the man's voice.

"You have to make your own chances here, Harrison. Bea just couldn't close the deal. She didn't have the drive to succeed in this world. All fluff and no substance on that one." Grace had no idea when to stop talking.

Jonas stopped and stared at the woman. "Nobody was asking for your opinion, Atwater. Bea might have been the best reporter this paper had. The paper never cared enough to see what she could do. Now she is gone." Without a word, he grabbed the notes the woman had meticulously taken the entire meeting. "She will be getting this interview, not you."

"She doesn't work here." She grabbed at the papers but missed.

"Then I will find where she's working, and that will be the paper that gets this article." He ripped the papers, and the woman visibly groaned at him as he tossed the pieces on the floor. Her big story was gone.

"See if anyone reads it now, Raiden. Nobody even cares about you and your company!" Atwater called after them as they headed out of the office and out of the building. He was half surprised when nobody chased after them.

"Sorry about that, Harrison. I know an interview was our best bet, but ..." He stopped and looked at his friend, who was just staring at him. "What?"

"Do you know where Bea is?" Harrison had his arms crossed but was grinning as he asked.

"No, but that's what my lawyer is for." Jonas got in the car with Harrison. It was the first time he had been outside his dad's house in days.

"You're in luck. I know exactly where she is." Harrison smiled as he slapped him on the shoulder, and the car took off.

"How do you know where she is?" he asked. Harrison seemed to know a lot about the woman.

"Because I'm married to her mother, and her mother keeps close tabs on her girls," Harrison stated.

"Bea is one of your stepdaughters? Why didn't you tell me?" he asked in shock. Though it did make sense that Buzz would be one of the wild girls that Emma had talked about so long ago.

"Because an hour ago, you hated her. There was no need for you to know where she was," Harrison admitted with a shrug.

"Who is she working for now? What paper?" Jonas demanded. He was going to give her the story she wanted—that she deserved.

"She isn't. She just sits at home with Agatha and Louisa most of the time. Wait, is Louisa your sister?" Harrison asked.

Nodding his head, he stated, "Yes. Has she has been with Buzz the entire time?"

"Since I got home from Hawaii, she has. Nice kid. I hadn't heard where they had picked her up." It sounded like his sister was a stray puppy to the family, and they might be keeping her.

"My house. I should have known she would go to Buzz."

"I thought she was stalking you, but you get to call her Buzz? I just started to get to call her that. Not a lot of people get to use that nickname." Harrison gave him a sideways glance.

"Louisa started calling her that, and then I did too," he lied.

Harrison pulled up in front of a large old house with Jeeps everywhere. Harrison got out of the car and walked up the steps, not caring if Jonas was following.

Following Harrison into the house, he noticed that all the shades were drawn, and the living room was completely dark, except for light coming from other parts of the house and now the open door. After closing the door behind him, he saw that there were close to a dozen pairs of eyes looking at them.

"Mom is at work," one of the faces said. Jonas had no idea which one.

"I know, I'm looking for Buzz," Harrison announced.

The entire group groaned and yelled, "Buzz!" at the top of their lungs. One of the group added, "She's upstairs." Jonas knew it was Louisa.

"Louisa, how are you?" She was snuggled into the corner of the couch next to another blonde.

"Okay. Having fun. I might have missed a week of school. Possibly my second," she admitted. Most of those in the room whispered that it was okay, and they were still proud of her.

Footsteps on the stairs turned his attention to the redhead coming down them. Today she was in a white V-neck T-shirt that said "BUZZZZ" in red across her breasts. When she saw him, her eyes went wide, and then she bit her lip in nervousness because Harrison was with him.

"Buzz, I got you an interview for an article," Harrison said.

"I'm not a reporter anymore. Give it to someone else." Buzz shook her head.

"My client wants you," Harrison reiterated.

"Ohhh, he wants *you*, Buzzy," someone said from the couch.

"Shut up, Maby." Buzz didn't move as she yelled back.

"Can I talk to you outside?" Jonas asked. Mostly, he wanted her away from all her sisters, who weren't even hiding the fact that they were listening to them.

"Her room is more private," someone stated.

"The neighbors won't call the cops about a little necking," another added.

"Gross! He's my brother," Louisa said.

"Get used to it, Lou. Lovelys are hard to resist." It was a man's voice. Jonas hadn't noticed a man in the group.

"Gross," another young voice replied.

"Emmaline, you are supposed to be in school."

A voice laughed. "Somebody's in trouble."

"Emma, we're going home right now. I'll take you so that Jonas and Buzz can talk." Harrison grabbed the teen by the arm and headed for the front door.

Watching him leave with his daughter, he wanted to do the same thing with Buzz, except he wanted her in a completely different way. He had forgotten everything she had lied to him about since they met. All he wanted was to hold her again, touch her again. He just wanted her in his arms.

CHAPTER TWENTY-FOUR

"OUTSIDE THEN." She didn't even know how she would be able to talk with him in the house. He filled her house as nobody had ever done before.

Without a word, she walked past him, grabbing a coat on her way outside into the afternoon sunshine. The bitter cold instantly made her shiver in her T-shirt. Her plan hadn't been to go outside at all that day, just like so many days before. Since coming home, she and Louisa had stayed put. How could Buzz make the kid do anything that she herself didn't want to do?

After hearing the door click behind them, she turned and said, "What do you want, Jonas?"

"I want you to write an article for me."

"As I said, I quit. Actually, I got fired, so I can't do that." She finally pulled on the coat.

"You can freelance," he argued.

"No, I'm done. Out of the game."

"Last week, you would do anything for a story, and now when it is handed to you, you don't even want it?"

"I wasn't working on a story last week." She rolled her eyes, not that he was ever going to believe her anyway.

"You weren't working on a story when you were hiding in my closet?"

"That wasn't last week; that was the week before. And anyway, once we slept together, I knew I couldn't write a story about you. I have integrity, and sleeping with my subjects is beyond even me." She folded her arms against the cold air.

"Then why were you following me around?" he asked.

"I wasn't following you. You just kept showing up." She argued.

"At the meeting?"

"The one that Lucy and Harper were catering? I help them out all the time."

"How did you know I was at the hotel?" His eyes were scrutinizing her as he asked.

"Okay, maybe I got that information from Sera, who accidentally said something about it to Harrison. I overheard it. That was the only time I did that. But in my defense, that was before I slept with you, so I was still trying to get a story then," she explained. It was true, and maybe she would do it again if the opportunity were presented to her. She probably just wouldn't sleep with the man this time. That's when things went sour.

"You worked at the house for a week."

"I wasn't there for you, and I had already been fired from the paper when I started that job. When you walked into the kitchen during my first day, I was in shock. I had no idea you lived there or was staying there or whatever you were doing there."

"You were working for George Raiden," he reminded her.

Cringing, she replied, "I was hired by Judith Rowley. I didn't know what her husband's name was. In no way did I ever think that she was your stepmom. I didn't do enough research about you to know who your parents are. It wasn't your past I was writing about; my story was about your uncle. I just wanted to get an interview to get my career out of the toilet, but instead, I only managed to get it flushed. So, I will not be doing an interview with you. I'm done with that."

"Why would you want to work for Judith if you're not even a chef or working on a story? Why would you do that to yourself?" he demanded.

Buzz was starting to get tired of his questions. "Just forget it. It's nothing that concerns you. After all, I'm nothing to you." She pushed him and went back into the house.

Except he grabbed her arm and stopped her. "Why were you there?"

Swallowing past the lump in her throat, she admitted, "I ... I wanted to find out something about Judith Rowley. Is that what you wanted to hear?"

"What could you possibly want to know about that woman? Did she steal your boyfriend? Brother? Was she sleeping with someone you knew? That seems to be what she liked to do."

"No, nothing like that. I didn't know she was sleeping around. Okay, I had some suspicions about her since I knew her past, but I thought she and George were kind of happy. How is George?" Her eyes met his. She had forgotten their father in all of this, that he had his heart torn by the woman.

"Dad's fine. He's finally getting a divorce like he's wanted for years. At least now he has the nerve to actually do it." He loosened his grip on her arm a little but didn't completely let her go.

A car door slammed in the distance, dragging her eyes from his, hating that he stopped liking her and she had just fallen more for him. Why couldn't she fall for someone who even liked her? Instead, she fell for someone she could never have.

"Jonas," a soft voice stated as a curvy young woman with shoulder-length brown hair with a thick purple streak walked right up to them.

The voice caused Jonas to turn to the woman, who looked them up and down and folded her arms. Jonas stiffened and frowned at her.

"Frances? What are you doing here?" he asked the woman.

The woman rolled her eyes at him. "You mean, picking up my sister after mother decided she wasn't good enough either? She called me a few days ago about Mom and some guys. Anyway, I finally got time enough to come and get her, so I'm going to take her back to Chicago."

Jonas frowned at her. "I'm taking her home; she doesn't need you. She belongs with Dad right now."

"Cute redhead." The woman nodded at Buzz as she said it. "Louisa needs to get away from everything right now. She needs a fresh start."

Instantly, Jonas dropped Buzz's arm and moved to block the door from the woman. Buzz couldn't decide what they were to each other, except that they didn't get along. That much was very obvious.

"Bea Lovely." She put her hand out to the woman in hopes of distracting her.

"Cute, you are lovely. Frankie Rowley." The woman took her hand and smiled. It was completely fake, and Buzz knew. She had seen that smile a million times over the years.

"My stepsister," Jonas provided but didn't seem very happy about it.

"Stepsister?" Buzz looked from one to the other.

"Soon-to-be ex-stepsister. I really like the sound of that, though I'll still be related to Judith in the end. You and George weren't the worst part of the family," the woman stated with a smile.

Buzz's mind was reeling. There was no doubt who this woman's mother was. "Holy fuck, how many kids did Judith have? How many more are there?"

"Just the two," Jonas answered the question. "Frances has been at reform school for the last few years."

"Frankie has *not* been at reform school; she's been at the U in Chicago, but do not tell my mother. I have no need for her in my life. Have you seen how well that turned out?" she argued.

Behind them, the door swung open, and a blast of warm air washed over Buzz. Harper stuck her head out and looked at the group, mostly at Frances, before saying, "I'm setting the table. How many are staying?"

"Nobody," Buzz said.

Frances shrugged at the invitation. "Just here for Louisa."

Harper yelled back into the house that three were staying and came out and shut the door to the house behind her. "What is she to you?"

It seemed that Harper was taken with her new little sister and was going to be as protective as she was with the rest of her sisters. It was cute to see, and she wished the girl herself was out here to see it, to know she was instantly part of the group.

"Her sister," Frances informed Harper.

Harper barely suppressed a laugh at the answer. "I don't believe you."

"Doesn't matter what you believe or not."

"Yes, yes it does. I'm Harper."

"Frankie."

"Full name, please," Harper demanded, as if there was a specific list of people who could enter the house.

"Frances Rowley."

"How old are you?" Harper barked out, as if the kid was trying to pull something over on her.

"Twenty-one, and you?" Frankie was not happy with the sudden inquisition.

"Thirty." Harper stared at her and then looked at Buzz and Jonas, then back to the young woman. "Well, come inside. Might as well get to know everyone."

"Why?" The woman asked her but followed. Probably because it was the easiest way into the house and to get her sister out of it.

"It's cold outside; only an idiot would stay in the cold. Don't be too overwhelmed." Harper smiled at Buzz and put her arm around Frankie, shutting the door behind them, leaving Buzz and Jonas alone again.

"What was that all about?" Jonas just looked at the closed door.

"Family stuff," Buzz said, loving how welcoming Harper was to their new sisters. Any number of them.

CHAPTER TWENTY-FIVE

WATCHING the door close behind the women, Jonas turned back to Buzz. "Back to you and Judith. What were you doing there?"

"I, um, went to work for Judith to see if she was my mother. Judith Rowley was her name," Buzz stated seriously.

Laughing, he touched her cold chin. "Aren't you happy that wasn't the case?"

Buzz just looked him in the eyes. "I was correct. She is my birth mother. Mine and my four sisters, and now your two sisters."

"Judith is your *mother*? How the hell does that happen?" His hand dropped. She had to be joking.

"She left us when I was four. We never saw her again until last week, when I ran into her at the paper after I got fired." She shrugged and took a step back from him.

"There is no way she is your mother," Jonas stated, because he had known the woman for twenty years, and she had never said anything about more than two kids. In fact, she barely tolerated those two.

"There's no way she's not, Jonas." She shivered, from the cold or from the fact that Judith was her mother, he didn't know.

"How long did you know? The entire time?" His mind went back to the many times he had kissed her in that house, touched her. Had she known then?

"Yes. Well, I thought so the entire time. Harper confirmed it when she met her." She looked at the house.

"Did Judith know it was you? Her kid? Or one of her kids because she had what, seven? Nine?" he gritted his teeth at the knowledge. That somehow, this woman was the daughter of his evil stepmother. How was that even possible?

"Just five more besides Louisa and Frankie. I don't think she realized who I was until she saw Harper. Harper looks a lot like Judith—and Louisa for that matter," Buzz informed him, and he started to see the resemblance.

"Why wouldn't she be excited to see you? I mean, it's been years." He knew asking her wouldn't give him the answers he needed since Buzz didn't know Judith at all.

"I don't think she ever told your dad about her other family. I'm almost certain she didn't."

"That woman just walked away from five kids and moved on to my dad? Leaving you and your sisters to be raised by your dad? Where did Frankie come from?" he asked. He had never heard anything about her father, just that he wasn't involved in her life.

"I don't know. Only Judith knows that."

"She abandoned you. Dad never even knew. Dad wouldn't have abandoned you if he'd known." Jonas hoped that was true, hoped it more than anything else he had ever hoped for. Because if not, his dad wasn't the person he had always thought he was.

"It turned out okay, Jonas. We got a great stepmom who treats us like her own. In fact, after meeting Judith, I'm happy she wasn't around."

"And you weren't there for me at all. You were there to find your mom. Why didn't you just tell me that? I asked you directly if you were there for a story, and said you were."

"Because when you asked me, Louisa was there, and I didn't want her to find out like that. Though it might have been better than my sisters blurting it out. But the group does make a lot of things easier."

"I should go in there and be with her during this. She's had a few bad months, and this is just the icing on the cake," he said and turned to do just that. If his sisters needed him, he should be there for them.

"Frankie is with her, so I think they're okay. If she had wanted to be with you, she would have called you. Instead, she called me, and then she called Frankie," Buzz said.

Ever since they were small, Frankie and Louisa had been polar opposites and usually didn't get along very well. A lot of it had to do with Judith's not hidden preference for the younger sister. Though George had tried over the years to correct that, he had no control over his wife and her treatment of them. It wasn't that they would fight, because that was not Louisa, but they would argue and go to their rooms.

Once Frankie had started to get in trouble at school, George and Judith had sent her to private schools in order for her to learn discipline, something that put a bigger wedge between the sisters. That only made Louisa their favorite even more in Frankie's eyes, making her lash out even more.

That she had called her sister meant that she wasn't planning on going home to George's house. It meant that she was mad at everyone, not just her mother.

"I think you're right. The sisters need to be together in this. If Louisa turned to Frankie, that's a good thing. They should turn to each other during hard times."

"They will always be your sisters, Jonas. Just give them time. This will blow over, and you guys will be a family again. Not the same as before, but still a family."

"A family that now includes you since you're my sister's sister? What does that make us? Buzz, we slept together, and you suspected we were related." He took a step back and glared at her. If she had just told him in the beginning, none of this would have happened.

"I tried and tried to stay away from you. You were the one that pushed," she reminded him.

"I wouldn't have if I had known. I see the apple doesn't fall far from the tree, does it. Like mother like daughter, using sex to get what you want. Well, it didn't work; I'm done with you," he stated angrily.

"I guess I am," she said without meeting his eyes, then opened the door. "I wish I didn't know that."

With that, she stepped into the house and closed the door. He could hear the women talking from inside and hoped his sisters were doing okay. But they were with their new sisters now—sisters that they needed to get to know.

Anger still seethed through him as he stood on the front step, wondering what had happened. Had the woman he had fallen for really just told him that they were related? It was through marriage, but it was still related.

"Did you get the interview, or were you just kicked out of the house?" Harrison asked as he walked up the steps.

"Interview is off, indefinitely."

"What happened? I can talk to Buzz if you need me to," Harrison said, pointing at the house.

"No, I need to get out of here and think," Jonas replied and realized that he had ridden with Harrison.

"I'll take you back to your dad's." Harrison wasn't pushing.

"That's okay; I'll walk. I need time alone," Jonas said. He needed to think and clear his head, and Harrison was the last person he wanted to talk to about it.

"So, no interview with anyone?" Harrison questioned.

"No. Harvey can talk all he wants, but the evidence shows what he did. I need to be as far from this as I can get for a while," Jonas decided, no longer needing to show his side. The evidence was on his side.

Just like with Buzz, the evidence pointed at her lying to him at every turn. Everything was just one big lie after another.

CHAPTER TWENTY-SIX

"Everyone, we need to talk," Buzz said an hour after leaving Jonas outside the house. Now she was walking into the living room with a bottle of water, two bottles of wine, and a case of wine coolers. She hoped it would be enough.

"In a minute," Lucy stated, her eyes not leaving the TV.

Setting down the alcohol, she handed the water to Maby, who gave her a dirty look. She hated being targeted as different. It had only come out a few months before that she had an issue with alcohol and was trying to stay away from it, not an easy task when you were a Lovely.

"Now, TV off," Harper barked at Lucy as she came in carrying as many glasses as she could.

"God, Harper, can you be a little nice? I was in the middle of that episode!" Lucy barked back at her sister. For a moment, Buzz thought they would start fighting over the TV. The tension between them was high and getting higher all the time.

"You've seen it before." Maby said from beside her. Her feet were on her twin, and her head was on her husband's shoulder. "We've all seen it before."

"It doesn't matter. I wanted to see it again." Lucy pushed her sister's feet off of her lap.

"Can I leave yet? Louisa and I need to get on the road," Frankie said. She was sitting on the arm of the couch, as close to the door as possible.

"I should pack." Louisa started to get up.

"Not yet. We're having a family meeting," Harper stated.

Agatha looked over at Harper. "Should I call Sera?"

"No, we can have a meeting without her."

"I don't think we can," Cliff stated as he played with his wife's hair.

"I'm not even calling Kaine for this. I'll give him a summary later." Harper grabbed the wine and started filling the glasses.

"Summary. Is that what you call it?" Agatha snarked.

"Shut up, Ag. I've always and will always call it sex. You know that." She handed her a full glass.

"Harper, really! There are kids here." Agatha took the glass and frowned at her sister.

"No, there aren't. Lou is like nineteen. If she doesn't know about sex yet, she should be informed." Harper handed the girl a glass of wine after just saying she was only nineteen.

"What are we meeting about?" Maby asked, handing her bottle of water to her husband to open, as if she was worthless.

"Louisa and Frankie," Buzz started.

"I don't need to be the subject of a meeting." Frankie got to her feet, declining a glass of wine.

Harper pushed her back onto the couch, as she would have with any of her sisters—no special treatment for the new ones. "First off, I have never had to do this before, not once. So, if I get it wrong, you'll have to tell me, though I'm usually far from wrong about anything. That's the first thing you'll learn about me."

"What are you talking about, Harper?" Maby demanded,

"Shut up, Maby. You're interrupting my speech," she hissed at her sister before turning back to the two newcomers. Clearing her throat, she went on, "As the oldest Lovely sister, I want to extend an invitation that you will always have a home here. No matter what happens in life, you belong here."

"Hold up, Harper. This is my place, not yours anymore. Need I remind you that you're supposed to be moved out since you are married and all. And I don't really know either one of them." Agatha sat up, suddenly caring about what was happening around her.

"I don't know any of you," Frankie agreed with Agatha and got to her feet again.

Harper pushed her down again. "You will in time." Harper then rapid-fire named everyone in the room as if the girl would pick up on any of the names.

"I'm not going to remember any of that," Frankie pointed out.

"I said in *time*, you will remember us all. Just give it time," Harper assured her, even patting her on the arm.

"Are you holding us hostage?" Louisa looked around the room at all the faces looking at them.

"I think you messed this up, Harper, completely," Buzz said and turned to the girls. "What Harper forgot to mention was that everyone in this room, except Cliff, is the daughter of Judith Rowley."

Louisa choked on her wine and looked around the room. "My mom?"

"Yup, our mom also. We haven't seen her since we were very young. I would say before Frankie was born," Buzz said.

"I don't see it." Lucy was analyzing them from behind her wine glass.

Her twin pushed her aside and sat on the coffee table, staring at them for a second. "Louisa ... Louisa May Alcott! Am I right? Little women? Little Men? I am so right!" She spun around and looked at her sisters as if they knew the answer. Well, two did.

Buzz nodded in agreement. "You're right. Her name is Louisa May Alcott Raiden."

Maby tried to get a high-five from Louisa, who just stared blankly at her. "Really? That's who I wanted to be, but no, I end up being Mabel Lucie Atwell Lovely. I never have any luck." Maby groaned and turned to Frankie, then smiled.

"You people make no sense," Frankie stated, shaking her head.

"Frankie ... Frankie, I got nothing. Seriously, I'm going to fail this one," Maby mumbled, and her husband leaned forward to pat her on the back.

"It's Frances," Harper said.

"Frances makes more sense. Okay Francis, Francis, F. Scott Fitzgerald—"

"Francis Elise Hodgeson," Frankie answered at the same time.

Maby recovered before Frankie could. "Burnett! I knew it. Of course, The Secret Garden. I was seriously thinking another damn illustrator." Maby popped up and rubbed the brunette's head as she walked away, her task complete.

"Did you want a shot at our names, or did you just want the tests over with?" Harper shot a look at Maby.

Buzz pushed Harper aside and explained. Based on the two sisters' expressions, they thought everyone in the room was crazy. Harper pushed back and said, "We all have long names, Frankie. Or really, we were all named after authors. I'm Nelle Harper Lee Lovely. Buzz is Beatrix Potter Lovely. Agatha is ..."

"Do not say it, Harper," Agatha cut in.

"You can look it up later. It's an easy one. Maby is Mabel Lucie Atwell Scott now, and her twin is Lucy Maud Montgomery Lovely."

"This doesn't prove anything," Frankie argued.

"It means you are a Lovely and will always be part of the family," Harper stated.

"I don't need any more family. I have Louisa." Frankie got up and turned to her sister.

"Frankie, come on," Louisa argued.

"No, Louisa. I don't need any more family like Judith. I've finally worked myself past being raised by that woman, and I'm not going to be rejected by these women also."

"They won't reject you. They're great." Louisa looked around the room. After all, she had been living with them for a few days now.

"I don't care. I'm leaving now, with or without you," Frankie stated.

Louisa looked around the room. Buzz knew she was torn. She loved her sister but really wanted to get to know the rest of the sisters. With her sister's words, Louisa finally got up from the couch and said, "I will get my stuff."

"I'll be in the car." Frankie fled the house.

"So, Judith popped out two more kids. Who saw that coming?" Lucy took a drink of her wine.

"What are we going to do about them?" Buzz asked the room.

"Nothing, they are adults and have to come to terms with this the way they need to. They know where we are," Agatha said, her glass already empty.

"But ..." Buzz started to argue. They shouldn't be leaving, not yet.

"Nope, it's not up to you. If you marry the brother, then they'll have to talk to you. You're sneaky about that." Harper tapped her hard shoulder with a fist as she said it.

"Not why I did it," Buzz mumbled, hoping no one else noticed, except they did.

"Sure, Buzzy, sure," Agatha said from her corner of the couch.

A few minutes later, when Louisa finally came down with a bag of stuff, most of which Buzz had borrowed her, everyone could tell she had been crying. With hugs all around, she finally left to go with her sister.

Buzz was sure she would see her again soon. Maybe not her sister, but Louisa. Unfortunately, she didn't think she'd ever see Jonas again. She had blown that out of the water ... big time.

CHAPTER TWENTY-SEVEN

Jonas turned away from his computer to look out the window. It was storming again, the second time this week. For weeks he had been practically living at work, and he didn't think that would change anytime soon.

It had been over a month since his uncle had finally broken down and confessed to stealing in order to cut a deal. It had been a great one for the old man. He was sitting in a cushy federal prison and would be there for five years. The company he had left behind was in shambles and would take a lot longer than that to get it back on its feet and gain the trust it had lost.

Jonas had made some great strides in that department, but only because he was working nonstop to make that happen. The more time he spent working, the less he thought about the redhead that was still on his mind.

His anger at Buzz had dissipated over the last month since he had last seen her. Looking back on it, he had realized that in the beginning, she was just doing her job ... just not conventionally. If he hadn't tried to scare her from the closet and had sex with her, she might have gotten an interview—an interview that he wished he had released before his Uncle Harvey had gone to the press, even if it hadn't helped him in the long run. Maybe Harvey wouldn't have fought it for weeks before giving up.

Now that he knew her real name, which was Beatrix Lovely, he had been able to find out so much more about her, including that her stepmom was indeed married to Harrison Dean. He would have known that if he hadn't skipped the wedding. Also, that her older sister, the one he had met as she made breakfast, was married to Kaine Hawthorn, one of the very companies that his uncle had stolen money from. On top of that, her other sister was married to Clifton Scott V of the Scotts and had money invested everywhere. Happily, not with Raiden & Son's Financial.

He had read every article she had ever published, and his sister had been right; nothing she had reported before was anything close to the scandal that his uncle had created. It seemed the woman had gone above and beyond to get his story. And failed.

After the night in his hotel room, she had never once asked him a question about his job. Not that she asked in the hotel room, but she had been distracted then, after all. It seemed she knew that after what had happened between them, she had to let go of that hot, juicy story, and she had.

Then she hadn't just blurted out her relationship to Louisa in front of the girl when she knew Louisa wasn't ready, letting everyone think she was after a story and not the genuine person she actually was. All to save Louisa's feelings.

After all that, he had told her she was just like her mother, a manipulative person who didn't have a heart. Buzz hadn't walked away from the one sister she barely knew; she had taken her in the moment Louisa needed her.

But he had burned that bridge, and no matter how much he wanted to rebuild it, he hadn't heard from her once. She was suddenly absent completely from his life. For weeks afterward, he had thought she would show up someplace: at work, on his jog, when he went shopping, somewhere. But nothing.

Now he was resigned to the fact that it was over, and he would never see her again.

"Hello, Son." George Raiden walked into the office, followed by Jonas's personal assistant on his heels.

From the panicked look on her face, it seemed the man just walked in, and she hadn't been able to stop him.

"Dad," he stated and smiled at Jill, letting her know it was okay.

"We have to talk, Jonas." His dad sat down and then didn't say anything, as if it had taken everything inside him to get him there and was done.

"Have you talked to Louisa lately?" Jonas asked.

Jonas hadn't heard from Frankie or Louisa since they'd gone to Chicago. Not that he really expected to. His relationship with Louisa was fragile, and with Frankie, nonexistent. All he knew was what his dad told him since Louisa had called him a few times.

"A week ago. She's looking for a job, but no luck so far," George replied absentmindedly.

"I can give her a job here. Both her and Frankie if they want them. They can move back in with you," Jonas said, something that he wished both his sisters would automatically know. There was always a place for them in the family company, and more importantly, in his life.

George's eyes instantly went to his lap. "No, they can't. I've decided to not stick around here anymore. The house is for sale."

"What?" Jonas sat up in his chair, shocked.

"Yes, decided this last week. There are just too many memories in the house, and I need a change. I'm moving to Belize," George replied, a little sheepishly in his admittance, still not meeting Jonas's eyes.

Jonas raised an eyebrow. "What's in Belize?"

"Sun, surf.... It's a nice place to retire." The older man shrugged.

"You've been retired for years. Why now?" The last time he had retired, he had moved here, as far from sun and surf as you could get.

"Judith—" his dad's voice cracked over the name, and then he cleared his throat and tried again, "Judith wants to move away from here also. She says that there are too many memories, and a fresh start is the best for us."

Jonas wondered if he was hearing things. It sounded like his father was taking back his lying, cheating wife—*again*. Not divorcing her like he had always said he wanted to do.

"You've been talking to Judith?" But he didn't have to ask, because his dad had just told him. It was so hard to believe.

George smiled a ghost of a smile and finally answered. "She showed up a few days ago out of the blue. We talked for a long time and realized where everything went wrong. We need a new start, a new start in a new place. We need to leave everything behind and focus on us being happy again."

"What about Louisa? Frankie? Her daughters?" he reminded his dad. Did they have a place in this new life?

"They're adults now, and they don't need us anymore. We can all get together for the holidays if you want to. Frankie hasn't needed us for years, and Louisa seems to be doing just fine without us. We can't just sit around waiting for our kids to come home; we want to keep living." George seemed to believe the words that he was saying.

Jonas leaned back in his chair. It seemed the woman had gotten her claws back into his dad. As he wondered how deeply, he asked, "You do know that she has five more kids, right? Kids that she abandoned when they were just little? Did she tell you that?"

"Of course, we have no secrets. Their father hid them from her for years. We spent a lot of money trying to find them, but no success. They were gone." George shook his head at their loss.

Jonas bit back the anger that his dad didn't deserve. It was his wife who had abandoned those kids and lied to her husband about them, though he wasn't going to let his father believe the lies anymore.

Leaning forward over his desk, he told the man the truth, "They have lived in the same house their entire lives, Dad. She knew exactly where they were. Some of them still live in that house. Their father abandoned them a decade later."

George shook his head at the revelation. "She doesn't know that. It would break her heart."

"Stop defending her, Dad. She showed her true colors, and you still don't see them. For a week, she knew that Bea was her daughter; she knew and didn't care. Not once did she actually talk to her. Even when her older sister was in the house, and Judith knew exactly who that daughter was. Still nothing," Jonas argued.

"She loves her kids, Jonas. She just has a hard time showing that love sometimes."

"You mean when she smothered your child for nineteen years and ignored Frankie? I know for a fact you saw that. And did you ever think to step in and protect Frankie? Once?" Jonas was just as mad at his dad for what had happened as he was at himself. He had chosen to not be there for his sister, and now he didn't think their relationship could be mended.

"I love Frankie. It's just her attitude that I have a hard time with," George argued.

"The one she adopted because her parents only paid attention to her when she acted up? Because her mother had chosen who was her favorite and who was not. Nothing she ever did was good enough for Judith. Or even you," Jonas said.

George huffed and straightened in his chair. "Not true."

"You know, I've always blamed how distant our family is on Judith, but you're just as much to blame as she is. You let her do whatever she wanted, even if it was harmful to everyone but her."

"You just don't understand, Jonas. You have never loved anyone enough to where their flaws don't matter, that you love them despite the fact that they have them. That's how I love Judith. She's my other half," the man said, as if he didn't spend years saying just the opposite.

"Why are you constantly separating from her then, trying to divorce her?" Jonas demanded.

"Because she can be a little annoying. But at the end of the day, I want to have spent that day with her. Once you find that love, you'll understand." He shrugged and leaned back in his chair.

"I understand love, and it's not giving a woman an oath of loyalty. Buzz has made mistakes, but she also takes complete responsibility for them. She doesn't make excuses for her actions that caused harm to others." He couldn't not think of that gorgeous redhead admitting why she said she did what she did, and it was for someone else.

"And Buzz is what?"

"I didn't say Buzz."

"Yes, you said Buzz made mistakes."

"Okay, fine, I said it. But ..." He stopped. He could say he didn't mean it, but he did. She may have her faults, but she owned up to them every time and put everyone first, taking everyone's feelings into account before her own.

George smiled at the answer. "Tell me about this woman who has captured your heart finally."

"Ask your wife, but she would know her as Beatrix," Jonas hissed, not wanting Judith anywhere near Buzz or anyone Buzz loved. Ever.

"The chef then? I could tell you were interested in her. Judith doesn't like when you mess with the help, but I think it can be forgiven this time." His dad grinned at him.

Jonas barked out a laugh. "No, Dad. She was never really a chef. She took the job in order to meet Judith, her mother."

"I don't think so." George looked uncomfortable, very uncomfortable suddenly.

Jonas smirked. "She's your stepdaughter, Dad. Don't you remember her from all those holidays? Or maybe because she has four sisters, you don't remember her specifically. She's the youngest."

"But ..." George had nothing more to say.

"But nothing. She was four when your wife walked out on her and her family. *Four*. Until the day she applied for the chef's job, Buzz hadn't seen her or even heard from her. Her name is Beatrix Lovely. You can ask your wife the rest of her kids' names. She might remember."

"You didn't sleep with her, did you? Your sister?" George demanded, as if George and Judith being married made them anything but strangers. The step between them was more like a cliff.

"Stepsister, Dad, and it happened before either of us were aware of our connection, which wouldn't have been an issue if you and your wife had introduced us at some point over the last twenty years. Or maybe I would have fallen in love with her anyway," Jonas said and knew it was true. He was in love with her. He had been for a long time now.

"But, Jonas, it's not right."

"It's more right than you forgiving that woman. Because she not only abandoned now seven children but also slept with two college students she invited to live in your house! One of which broke your daughter's heart!" Jonas reminded him of what had driven them apart.

George scoffed. "That wasn't what it looked like."

Jonas shook his head at his poor, gullible father. "I think you need better glasses because I saw exactly what was happening."

"They ..." he started to explain.

"You can stop talking. I don't care what she told you. There's no excuse for anything she has done. She has a history of abandoning her kids, and you are going to do the same. I never thought you would do something like that," Jonas told him and watched him pale at the words.

"I am not abandoning them." George got to his feet in anger.

Jonas followed suit. "Yes, you are. I just hope you follow your wife's lead and never come back. We will be fine without you."

"You just don't understand, Jonas." George's shoulders slumped at the words, letting Jonas know that he was choosing his wife and not his kids. He may have been able to deny it when he walked into the office, but not anymore.

"You got that right, Dad, and I never will." Jonas shook his head at the man. He didn't know him anymore. "Bye, Dad."

His dad only mumbled something Jonas couldn't understand as he walked out of the office and out of Jonas's life.

CHAPTER TWENTY-EIGHT

Six weeks later, and so much had changed. Buzz was back to being employed, if you could call it that since it was a petty job from Kaine and his Marketing Director/sister-in-law, Bex Carter. It was going better than she had thought it would. So far, she had made seven press releases, and all had been run in the paper she had nearly begged to get something printed at for over a year.

It should have made her feel ecstatic, but she couldn't bring herself to be happy. It was just a reminder that she couldn't do it by herself.

Sera had moved out and surprisingly stayed out, though Emma had moved back in five times. Each time, her dad had moved her back in with them—no lecture at all. The transition had been rough on them all, it seemed. Harper and Maby were staying at their new homes more and more. Over the last week, neither had stayed at the house overnight.

On a positive note, Agatha hadn't spent one night away from the house. So far, she hadn't found a new job, and nobody was telling her she needed one. Buzz thought that she was just as freaked out about the situation of there only being three of them living in the house as she was. They didn't talk about it, though, because that would be admitting something.

Lucy had quit working with Harper completely since the wedding. Not slow and gradual, but abruptly. Harper was now hiring more people to help her, not relying on family at all. That included another chef and four wait staff. Lucy and Harper were not talking about it; in fact, they weren't talking about anything anymore. Their once-close friendship had ended, and without the big blow-up Buzz had always thought would end it. Just a puff, and it was gone.

That meant the entire household had changed. There was almost no laughing, and barely anyone talked. Life had changed.

Or maybe nothing had changed, just how Buzz saw it. Her ambition and drive for life were gone. She had fallen in love for the first time in her life, and it had been with the wrong person, the wrong man.

A knock on the door made her groan. She didn't want to talk to anyone, she didn't want a lecture, and she didn't want company.

"What?" she barked in anger.

Instead of an answer, Harper poked her head in the door and looked at her. "Want to talk?"

"No." She closed her eyes and regretted staying in Harper's room. She should have moved to the master weeks ago, but that would require ambition, and her's was gone. Instead, Lucy had moved in and was never going to leave now.

"Too bad." Harper barged into the room and sat on the edge of the bed, leaning over Buzz and blowing on her face until she opened her eyes in annoyance. "Talk to Harps about it, Buzzy."

"Just leave me be." Buzz pushed her way from her.

"It's either talk or kick you out of my room."

"Does Kaine know about your attachment to this room? Shouldn't you be attached to his bedroom?"

"Oh, he knows of my attachment to his room and him, but he knows why I keep this one. We talk about stuff." Harper shrugged.

"No, you do not."

"Well, we do now. I've let him in, and now he knows way too much. Hell, he can even predict what I'm going to say sometimes. It's annoying as hell." She scrunched up her face at the admission.

"He shared a womb with Mom. Isn't that weird for you?" Buzz tried another tactic that was sure to piss off the blonde and send her away.

"I expected better from you, now that you've dipped into that same pool—and liked it," Harper rambled and then stopped and touched Buzz's chin with her finger. "Loved it *and* him."

"Don't remind me. I have to get over him and get on with my life."

"How's work? Bex won't say," Harper said.

Buzz didn't know if it was because Harper wouldn't ask or because Bex really wouldn't tell her. The two had gotten off on the wrong foot and had yet to become more than enemies, even if they were married to siblings. Everyone else got along with both of them equally.

"Good, it's a job. I think I'm doing well at it. Bex is fun to work with; she really knows her stuff, even if she only just started as the director. Yesterday, Arabella brought in the twins. They're adorable," Buzz gushed.

"They are. Can you believe I have three nieces and nephews? Harper shook her head at the thought.

"Do you think Maby and Cliff or Mom and Harrison will start first?" Buzz wondered out loud.

Harper winked and said, "Sera is actively working on it, so I say them. But Maby has surprised me on enough occasions, so I wouldn't put it past her." Then she added, "Have you heard from Lou or Frankie?"

"Louisa calls every so often. Never Frankie. But they're together and doing okay. Louisa might try school again in the fall. Not in literature this time, but marketing. I told her to come back here for it since Judith is gone, and we have a bedroom. We could teach her to be a Lovely. From what she tells me, Frankie already is one, though Frankie is a computer nerd, so she's a little different from us."

"What does she say about Judith?" Harper asked.

"Nothing, and I don't ask. She's going through a lot right now, and probing her about Judith won't help that. Hurting her to make me feel better just doesn't feel right," Buzz admitted. She longed to know things, but the younger girl wasn't ready to be asked yet. Maybe in time.

"What do you want to know?"

"Just stuff."

"Like what?" Harper pulled her feet under her, getting comfortable.

"Like, why did she leave? I don't remember her leaving. Did she say goodbye? Did she take one last look at us before she left? In my heart, I always thought she didn't want to go but was forced to. That there were things beyond her control that made her leave us behind— for our safety or something. Like a movie." Buzz smiled at the thought, except after meeting the woman, she knew that it was just selfishness that made her leave.

"I think she just got what she wanted and walked away. A month before she left, she got her doctorate. I remember Dad celebrating it; we had a cake and everything," Harper said. All these years, she had known, but Buzz had never asked, afraid of the answer. "I think she used Dad for a free education. She was here for around ten years, just about the right amount of time for it. I don't know if Dad realized.

"I had always thought that if we ran into each other, she would hug me and tell me why she left, then apologize for what she did to me and to everyone. But when she knew it was me, she told me to leave. She didn't care that it was me and wanted me out of her life again." It had hurt at the time, and it still stung.

"She didn't say goodbye; she just walked out the door and never came home. She didn't love anyone, Buzzy. Not even Lou got her real love. She just used her to get what she wanted. George had money, and Judith wanted that. I don't even know if Louisa is his. Seems convenient that she got pregnant," Harper mused.

"You don't know that. You're just making it up."

"I am, but it's the only way I can explain why she stayed. If there hadn't been money, she would have walked away from Louisa years ago. It seemed after she found George, she wasn't able to shake Frankie. I wonder if she ever thought to drop her off here. We would have taken her in. I mean, it's not like we were all Bradford's anyway," Harper stated as she shrugged.

"Who's not Dad's?" Buzz asked, sitting up. It was something nobody ever brought up, but it was always there.

"Agatha for sure," Harper said, and then tapped her fingers on Buzz's stomach for a while, like she was thinking. "And others maybe."

"Me, right? You don't think I am Dad's?" Buzz demanded in anger, swatting her hand away from her stomach. Why would it be obvious that she wasn't Bradford's? Red hair was a recessive gene that would show up anywhere, anywhere!

Harper got defensive right away. "I did not say that. I said others. Others could be anyone."

"You?" she questioned her oldest sister.

Harper used her "know it all" voice to explain. "Well, I am the first born, historically called the one that was surely his."

"Historically, my ass. Maybe he just took you in when Mom came. Ever think about that? That he married her, knowing that you were not his and decided to raise you anyway?" Buzz pointed out.

"Um, no. That's not true." Harper shook her head in denial.

"No, no, this makes sense. You're named after an adult fiction writer, then Lucy a youth, and Maby is a youth illustrator, then me, another youth," She pointed to herself. "And Agatha is back to adult. Pattern says you and Agatha are the ones not his."

"Except he was not a children's lit professor; he was adult, making Agatha and me the sure bets." Harper pointed out with a smugness only she could pull off during this discussion.

"Except you pointed out Agatha was not, so your theory is flawed," Buzz argued.

"What theory?" Agatha asked from the door. "The one that involves me."

"Nothing, Agatha. I just said you are not," Harper hissed at her sister, causing Agatha to come further into the room.

"Paternity, who can claim Dad," Buzz said, and Harper slapped Buzz's hip.

"Oh, that. That's easy," Agatha said and turned to leave.

"Stop and tell us then!" Harper jumped up, grabbed her, and pulled her back into the room.

"Only two of us can claim that they share a father," Agatha stated with confidence. Like everyone should know the information.

Harper sat up straight and demanded, "Did Mom tell you that? How do you even know?"

Agatha smiled. "Because I have spent my life with you people. I know you better than you know yourself."

"So, me and you then, Agatha? My theory stands. Sisters forever!" Harper shot her hands in the air, proclaiming victory.

Agatha laughed at her reaction and shook her head. "You think we share a father but not the identical twins?"

"So, nobody?" Buzz surmised, because the twins, of course, shared a father. Even Judith couldn't break that rule.

"And nobody is Dad's. He knew it the whole time, but Judith had something over him that made him accept every one of us. Not love us, but accept us. Then he walked away the moment he felt he could."

"How do you even know?"

"Dad told me." She shrugged, as if their dad had been all chatty about things.

"You are such a liar. I can't even believe I believed you for even a second. You were eleven when he left. Why would he tell you anything?" Harper demanded of Agatha.

"Because I asked why none of us looked alike. He answered," Agatha said and headed for the door. "If you want him as your daddy, he is. Because he's as close as you will ever get to your actual one."

With that, Agatha was out the door and stomping up the steps to her room, the heavy footfalls announcing to the house that she was not accepting company for the rest of the evening.

"Do you believe her?" Buzz asked.

"I don't know. Probably. Then again, it doesn't matter. Like she said, there isn't going to be some guy who will actually want the job now."

"Do you think he thinks about us as much as we think about

him?" Buzz asked, sitting back on the bed, realizing how much time she had spent wondering about her birth parents over the years.

"I don't know. Maybe." Harper turned to her.

"Do you think he would have been happier never knowing about his kid? That it was just something that tied him to a woman he hated and nothing else? Just a reminder of a bad time? One he couldn't even bring himself to love?" Buzz whispered, a tear slipping from her eye as she curled into a ball on her bed.

"Buzzy, what are you talking about?" Harper sat back down.

"I'm pregnant, and I know the father hates me—hates me a lot. He's going to hate the baby too, just like Dad did." She wiped away the tears in anger.

"Or he could be waiting for you to make the first move because he's as scared of rejection as you are. Baby Buzzy makes the perfect excuse to reach out." Harper tapped Buzz's stomach again.

"He isn't. You didn't see his eyes when he said I was just like Judith. He hates me, and he's right. I am just like her." Buzz buried her head in the pillow.

"You are if you never actually tell a man he is the daddy and give him the option of being a daddy. Because in twenty-some years, do you want your daughter to be having this same talk with someone about who her dad is and if he loved her or even wanted her? Or if her mom robbed her of that relationship for being scared?" Harper started to braid Buzz's hair as she talked. It was something she used to do before Sera came to live with them.

"I'm not scared. I know the answer," she admitted but didn't move. If she moved, Harper would stop.

"Then do the right thing and tell him. If he doesn't want the baby, have him put that on paper. Baby Buzz is going to want proof some-day. After all, she is the daughter of a great reporter." Harper's fingers stopped braiding and pulled her hair until Buzz had to slap her hands away.

"You're right. Legally, I have to give him an out." Buzz nodded; she had to let him decide, let him be the one to reject his child. She couldn't do that for him.

"Of course, I'm right; I'm Harper." She slapped Buzz on the ass and walked from the room. Then poked her head back in and added, "I put some leftovers in the fridge for you swinging singles."

With that, Harper was gone, and the house was silent again. Lucy was either out or quiet in her room. Agatha was in her room, but just as quiet.

Buzz headed down to the couch and TV to get away from the suddenly too quiet house. She was starting to dislike the house for its constant silence. She missed what it used to be like, even if she had no place to sleep. At least then, there was no silence.

CHAPTER TWENTY-NINE

"Jonas, Harrison Dean is here. Do you have time to see him and his client?" Jill, his personal assistant, said into the phone. She wasn't twenty feet from him but still called for things like this.

"I am his client, and yes, I have a few minutes," he said to her, wondering what his lawyer is doing there. It had been weeks since he had needed to see him for anything.

Perhaps it had to do with his dad leaving the country. He set his pen down. Their conversation had been three days ago, and so far, he was sure his dad was still planning on leaving the country with his wife. Or already had; Jonas wasn't communicating with him anymore.

After George had walked out of his office three days ago, Jonas had spent time on the phone with another lawyer: his dad's. Jonas wanted to make sure that Frankie's and Louisa's trust funds were intact and still had funds in them. Neither could withdraw anything from them until they were twenty-five, except to pay for college, so Jonas had set up an additional trust with his own money to get them by until then. Unlimited funds for each to do what they wanted with. There was no way either of his sisters would be left destitute by their parents' abandonment.

Harrison walked in with his arms folded, and a frown was set on his face. Close behind him was Buzz, dressed from head to toe in black, from her pumps up to her tight-fitting slacks and black blouse. All the black did was extenuated her red hair that was in a chignon, which hid the curls he knew were there. His fingers were already itching to touch her again.

"Morning, Jonas. My client is here, and she just needs a signature." Harrison didn't sit, just leaned against the wall at the edge of his desk. "My client, Beatrix P. Lovely."

"Uhm, thank you for seeing me, Jonas," Buzz said. All the confidence she'd had in that closet months ago seemed to have vanished.

"Beatrix, Jonas Raiden is also my client. Therefore, I will represent both of you during this." Harrison shook his head and nearly growled.

"I can represent myself today, Harrison. She is your stepdaughter, and I don't want to put you in the middle of this," Jonas stated, wondering what exactly *this* was about. Buzz was sweating, and Harrison was pissed.

"No, you're both my clients today. You can think about another lawyer tomorrow—you'll need one. I've drawn up all the appropriate documents that you have requested. Against your lawyer's advice, I might add. All you need to do is sign," Harrison said, pulling a paper from his red folder and setting it on the desk in front of Jonas.

In confusion, Jonas picked up the papers, the ones he hadn't even known about, much less requested to be drawn up. Looking at it, he couldn't make any of it make sense.

"It's just a standard affidavit of Voluntary Relinquishment of Parental Rights, a document stating that you will relinquish your paternal rights as of today. It's just a formality, really, but I don't want to have you thinking that you need to be a part of the baby's life or that I want anything from you. We'll be fine," Buzz stated, more calmly than she felt.

Dropping the paper as if it had burned him, his eyes went to Buzz's face. "*Baby?* You're pregnant?"

"My client is seven weeks pregnant. If you insist on a paternity test before signing, you will have to wait until the birth, per request from my client, Beatrix P. Lovely," Harrison stated for her, as if she couldn't talk.

"It's mine? Of course, it's mine, or you wouldn't be here," Jonas choked out.

"Once again, paternity tests will not be conducted until the baby is born," Harrison repeated.

"How long have you known? Weren't you going to tell me?" Jonas demanded in anger, pushing the paper away. He didn't want to see it anymore.

"Buzz, you said you told him and that he wanted to sign the paper." Harrison glared at Buzz.

"I knew he wouldn't want a baby with me. And I don't want my baby to grow up like me, with a dad who can't love her. Once he signs the paper, she will know that it was her dad who didn't want her, not that her mom fucked up so badly that she never got to know who he was. She deserves better than that," Buzz told Harrison, but Jonas saw a tear fall from her eyes before she angrily wiped it away.

"Buzz, you told me he had already agreed to this! You lied to me, your lawyer! You asked me to be your lawyer, and I agreed, and you lied to me." Harrison was madder than Jonas was at that point.

Buzz's jaw set with sudden determination. "Harrison, I am not going to trap him in something he doesn't want. I am going to end things now before there's a chance that her little heart gets broken because her father doesn't want her. I never want her to feel that pain —not for one moment. This will get done before she even knows it happened."

"Is it a girl? A daughter?" Jonas asked, his eyes on Buzz, seeing if there were any changes in her body. He couldn't see any. She was as perfect as she had been before.

Visions suddenly rushed through his mind: Buzz pregnant, very pregnant as she held up an impossibly small outfit that their baby would one day wear. That morphed into her holding on to a toddler with chubby arms and legs and red curly hair; her head rested on Buzz's shoulder, content. Then to that same red-haired girl running to him as he walked in the door, laughing as she came, her mom behind her walking slower but smiling still. Then they came in quick succession: the girl in braces, in her first car, graduating, getting married, all with Buzz beside him for every event. Together.

"I don't know. I just feel like it is." Buzz turned to him, and he saw how scared she was in her eyes. "Just sign it, and I will leave. You will never hear from me again. I swear."

"Or her?" Jonas asked, his eyes dipping to her stomach, the one that carried his baby. The visions suddenly changing, and he was suddenly not there for any of it. He was missing his life.

She visibly swallowed and nodded, and another tear ran down her cheek. "Her too."

"Why are you telling me? I would have never known if you hadn't walked in here," he asked, wondering why she was going through this.

"I don't want my baby to grow up like me, wondering what she did so wrong that nobody loved her or how her parents could walk away and never look back. Why was she so unlovable that they could just leave and not care? One day she will ask, and I will be able to show her you weren't interested. I just hope that I can love her enough so that she won't care," Buzz said through constant tears, then looked up at Harrison and smiled. "Like Sera did for my sisters."

"Harrison, you can tell your client that I will not be signing this paper, not now and not ever. I will never *not* be a part of our daughter's life, not for one moment."

"Jonas, be reasonable. I know you hate me and will never forgive me. What I did was unforgivable. I'm a monster—like mother, like daughter, after all. But I assure you that I will never walk away from my baby. She's already loved so much. You can just go on with your life without us," she said.

"Buzz, I will *never* sign away my rights to my child."

"But ..." Her face drained of color right before his eyes.

"But nothing, Buzz. You thinking I wouldn't want to be a part of her life makes me wonder if you even knew me at all. I may not get along well with my family, but I love them. And if you think for one moment that I'll let you deprive me of knowing my child, you're mistaken. I have rights, ones I will exercise if I have to," Jonas replied, crumpling the paper on his desk and tossing it towards the garbage. It missed and bounced onto the floor.

Harrison stared at him and then grabbed Buzz by the arm, forcing her out of the chair and out of the room. Everything had just gotten completely out of hand, and Jonas wondered what was going to happen now.

"Harrison, you're my lawyer!" he called after the man.

"Not anymore, Jonas. Now I'm part of her family, and as such, I will protect her from people like you," his friend since college stated and slammed the door closed as they left.

When the door banged shut, the sound knocked something loose inside of him, or maybe it was the realization of what he did. He had just let the woman who he was in love with, who was carrying his baby, walk out of his office in pain and in fear. Because of him.

CHAPTER THIRTY

It had been almost twenty-four hours since she had talked to Jonas, and so far, he hadn't reached out to her, in person or through his lawyer—his new lawyer.

Harrison had said they couldn't do much until they heard what Jonas was going to do. No matter what, they were going to fight it.

Or so Harrison thought, but they weren't. If Jonas wanted to be a part of the baby's life, she would let him. A child needed to know both her parents. Buzz had been raised without that and wanted better for her own child.

Until then, she would wait, and if waiting meant helping Harper prepare for a wedding she was catering the next day, then she would. Even if she was going to do it from the living room with a movie on.

"Okay, we're having a meeting about this situation," Harper stated as she walked down the stairs. Buzz was sure she had been checking on her bedroom, but Buzz wasn't sure why.

"What situation?" Lucy asked as she walked in from the kitchen, already eating ice cream from the container she was holding. Despite being in the same house, the two weren't speaking, and Lucy wasn't helping Harper any more than Buzz was.

"The baby situation," Harper replied and joined her on the couch.

Lucy squeaked something and dropped the ice cream container onto the floor just as Sera burst into the house. Tears were already in her eyes as she rushed to Buzz's side. It seemed Harrison had told his wife; so much for lawyer-client confidentiality.

"Buzzy, are you okay? You look okay, but are you really? Harrison didn't tell me anything had happened yet, but don't worry. We will fight him about this until we bring him to his knees," Sera said as she hugged Buzz to her chest, a little too close to the woman's breasts for Buzz's comfort. Actually, none of it was comfortable for Buzz, so she shook the woman off.

"I am fine; we are not fighting it. If he wants to be in the baby's life, I can't stop him." Who was she to deny a child their father?

"No, he gets nothing. This baby is our baby, and I will do everything in my power to keep it away from him," Sera announced.

"Sera, he's the dad. I can't change that. He has rights." Buzz shook her head.

"What is this meeting about? Are we now getting texts about them?" Maby said while walking into the house, which was easy since Sera had left the door open as she'd rushed inside.

"Buzz's baby," Sera stated, tapping Buzz's still flat stomach.

"Buzz's baby," Lucy said on a semi-hysterical laugh and then shoved ice cream into her mouth.

"What about this baby? Are we happy, or are we concerned? I need some direction on this." Maby took off her jacket and hung it up.

"The father wants his rights," Sera replied in disgust as Buzz's phone rang in her pocket.

Checking the screen, she saw it was Louisa. The girl hadn't called often, which meant Buzz always picked up when she did. Putting up her hand, she answered and went into the living room to talk to her. The drama of Buzz's life would have to be on hold for a moment.

"Buzz, are you there?" the younger woman's voice came over the phone.

"I'm sorry, I had to get away from the sisters. What's happening?"

"It's just that I need you. Can you please come and get me?"

"Where are you? In Chicago?"

"No, I came back a few days ago. Mom and Dad are staying together, but they're leaving us behind. Can you come? I need someone to talk to," she said, a bit calmer than Buzz felt.

George was back with Judith? After she had cheated on him? After she had said what she had to Louisa? What was wrong with him?

What did Judith have over that man that made him weak enough to take her back? It was probably the same thing she'd had over Bradford for years. It seemed Judith had some kind of magic over men. Buzz wished for a second that she had a little of that, then dismissed the thought. It was what probably made the woman evil.

"Yeah, text me the address, and I'll be there in a few," Buzz promised. Her sister needed her way more than Buzz needed "talk" she was about to get.

Back out in the living room, everyone was arguing about what Buzz should be doing. And some of it involved moving out of state.

"Louisa is in town, and I have to go talk to her. Her parents are back together," Buzz announced to the group, which made all the planning stop completely.

"Her parents, like Judith and her dad?" Maby asked in disgust.

"I guess. I have to go talk to her. I don't know how long it will take, so meeting dismissed, I guess," she said. The meeting thing was new since they used to all just live together. Now half of them were gone, and there were meetings—mostly spur-of-the-moment meetings at that.

Deciding she wasn't going to change for this, Buzz grabbed her coat and walked out of the house in pink sweats and a matching "Buzzzz" T-shirt. Or she would have believed they matched if Agatha hadn't pointed out earlier in the day that they didn't.

Across town, she checked the address again to make sure that the big house in front of her was the one she was looking for. Not that she had wondered where she was meeting the girl when she had left the house. Getting out of the Jeep, she walked up to the front door and rang the bell, hoping that she had the right place.

"Buzz, you came!" Louisa said and opened the door. Buzz was surprised at how much she liked the modern aesthetics of the house.

"You asked, so sisters come," Buzz said and shrugged off her jacket. "How are you doing?"

"Okay, it seems just weird that Dad would do this. I wasn't surprised with Mom since she'd walked away from you five. So why not me too? But Dad? I always thought Dad would be there for me."

"I understand. I never thought George would do something like that," Buzz said. "What are you going to do now? Where's Frankie?" Buzz looking around but didn't see the other woman.

"I'm looking at going to school in the fall, but I don't know where. Frankie isn't sticking around Chicago, and she's graduating. So, I have to start planning something," Louisa sighed.

"There is always room at the Lovely house if you need a place to stay. Frankie too. The more, the merrier, and you'll each get your own room," Buzz added, but she was in no way living with more people than beds again. Couch surfing got old fast.

"We'll talk about it. I just don't know what I want to do at this point. I feel lost," Louisa said, and she seemed like it.

"I know the feeling. I'm lost as well," Buzz admitted, even if she hated to. She was completely lost.

"But you have Jonas, so you'll be okay." Louisa patted her back.

"Uhm, that's over now. Didn't he tell you? We've been over since I last saw you," Buzz said, not mentioning the baby, though Louisa would find out sooner or later since she was related to both of them.

"He didn't," Louisa answered. "He said something completely different, in fact."

With that, Louisa got up and stomped into the kitchen and started talking low to someone. Buzz had no idea whose house they were in, but it must be some sort of friend of Louisa's. It was probably the homeowner; this was no rental. Or at least not a rental a nineteen-year-old could afford.

Following the younger woman into the kitchen, her steps faltered when she saw Jonas talking to his sister. He was in jeans and a T-shirt that made his muscles pop. Damn him and his muscly good looks. Even after everything that had happened, they were mouthwatering.

Buzz immediately took a step back, sensing a trap. Louisa had been in on it, but she hadn't known the real reason Jonas had asked her to help him. Hell, Buzz didn't know the reason.

She made it to her Jeep without him catching her. She had been willing to fight her way out, and she was very skilled at fighting after being raised in the Lovely house.

As she drove home, she let the tears fall. He had no right to do that, to use his sister to get to her. Louisa didn't deserve that.

No matter the reason he wanted her there.

CHAPTER THIRTY-ONE

"Is THERE a reason I was nearly run down by a redhead in a Jeep?" Frankie asked as she walked into the kitchen on her way back from some errand she needed to run, though she wouldn't say what.

Jonas couldn't see her because Louisa was holding him hostage with a sharp little fist and an amazing right hook—a right hook that had sent him to the floor with one swing.

"Yes, Jonas is an ass," Louisa stated from above him, her fist raised.

It was when Louisa had punched him that he'd realized he had made a mistake. He should have just talked to his sister about his plan. It had been a great plan that had fallen into place since the two sisters were already in town to pack up Louisa's remaining stuff from George's house. It was just a stroke of luck that they had asked him if they could stay with him for the night. He had needed their help in this.

But things hadn't turned out as planned. Not at all.

"I thought I was the only one who thought that," Frankie said and looked over the island at him and chuckled until she saw that his eye was turning colors. "Did the redhead hit him?" Her voice even sounded sincere.

"No, I did. He lied to me to get her here." Louisa grinned at what she had done, proud of herself.

"So, this wasn't a little family reunion?" Frankie waved her hand around, which made the dozen bracelets on her wrist clink noisily.

"No, he wanted me to lure her over for some nefarious reason." Louisa nearly hit him again as he tried to sit up.

Holding up his hands in protection, he said, "Not some nefarious reason, I wanted to talk to her and tell her that I love her."

"Oh, he *loves* her," Louisa mocked.

"I do, and she won't talk to me on my own."

"Have you tried? She's actually very easy to talk to," Louisa stated, finally relaxing her fists and then checking out the back of her hands in amazement.

"Jonas is more used to screwing her," Frankie said as she sat down on an island stool.

"How do you even know? You weren't even there," he asked his sister, who now had the most unbecoming shade of blue hair.

She shrugged. "I hear things. Mostly from this one, so stop getting caught at it."

"I happen to be in love with her," he announced to both of them.

"So, you keep saying to me, but do you say it to her? Because I think she might be more interested in that information than me. I'm a bit put off by it. I mean, you're supposed to be my brother, and she's kind of my sister. You're stepping into the icky there." Frankie made a face of disgust.

"I can't talk to her, so I can't tell her. She happens to live in a house surrounded by a half dozen overprotective sisters," he said, knowing exactly where she was.

"That's just an excuse. There are only three that live there now: Lucy, Agatha, and Buzz, which is the same amount you have here. Yet you're sitting on the floor afraid of a nineteen-year-old that wouldn't hurt a fly. Unless you hurt her sister; then it seems she will pop you in the eye." Frankie laughed and mimicked a punch.

"I'm not afraid of her." He didn't look at her either in case she popped him in the other eye. She had really surprised him with the first, which was how Buzz was able to get out of the house without him catching her and talking to her.

But Frankie was right; he knew where she was. He had known all along. All he had to do was knock on her door ... and probably get another black eye from another sister. Then maybe he'd get to talk to Buzz. It was just a toss-up at that point.

"I think that's a dangerous house for me right now," he said.

"You think, Jonas? You got her pregnant and then walked away," Frankie stated, making Louisa's eyes pop. He hadn't informed her of either.

But if he hadn't, and Louisa hadn't, who had? Was Frankie talking to Buzz or even another sister?

"I didn't know until this week, and I told her I wanted to be in the baby's life. And Buzz's," He hurried to tell Louisa as he watched her fists clench again.

"If you already told her, why do you need to tell her again?" Louisa demanded, looming over him.

With his arms up again in protection, he stated, "I didn't actually tell her I wanted her, just the baby. But neither of you were there. I just found out I was going to be a father."

"So what? This family is full of people who don't actually care about being around. Why would you want to be?" Frankie asked.

"Because I am not my father, or yours, or Buzz's. I just want to be a dad and spend my life with the woman I fell in love with. Be a family," Jonas said from his heart.

"Go get her then," Frankie replied with a grin. It seemed he had finally won her over.

"And don't mess up," Louisa added, reaching out a hand to him.

Grabbing it, he asked, "Will you two come with me and have my back?"

"Fight with my sisters?" Frankie asked as if she had never done that with Louisa.

"Possibly." He couldn't say it wouldn't happen; he was sure it would.

"I'm in if Muhammad Ali there is." Frankie pointed at Louisa, whose only answer was an enthusiastic nod.

His sisters were backing him on this, but they might side with their new sisters if push came to shove. On the drive over, they seemed enthused about the prospects of battling every woman in that house in order to find the one he loved. It seemed they were both into romance at the moment, and this operation had taken on an air of a fairy tale—a written one, of course, or so Louisa had informed him as she patted him on the head.

Pulling to a stop outside the house Buzz lived in. The house he hadn't been to since the day he had found out she was his stepsister. That was when his nerves started to catch up with him. Maybe Buzz didn't want him in her life; maybe she was happy with how they had parted.

And perhaps his two young sisters were not who he should have brought for this operation. In the house, all the lights were blazing, which meant the house was probably full of people. Maybe even husbands who would kill for their women.

Out of the car and into the cold night, he walked up the front steps and onto the porch before knocking on the door. Within seconds, the door flew open, and the teenager from lunch so long ago looked him up and down and said dryly, "You're not the pizza guy."

Then she slammed the door in his face before he could even respond. Not that he had a response planned for that.

Knocking again, he was sure that the kid was telling everyone he was there, and they were mobilizing.

"Maybe you should get pizza and bring it back. I didn't think of a distraction before. I think you need a distraction," Frankie said from behind him.

"Go back to the car. I'll tell you if I need you," he hissed at her.

"But then we'll be way far away in the car, unable to help," Louisa said. "I like the pizza idea."

Before he could shush them again, the door opened once more, and the same teenager looked at them. She held the door open wide and yelled, "See? I told you it wasn't the pizza guy. Just that guy Buzz let get her prego."

Then she slammed the door on him again, except he was quicker this time and put his foot out to stop the door from actually shutting. When it bounced off his shoe, he pushed his way into the house.

Yes, he knew he was trespassing, but the teenager wasn't letting him in, and nobody else would answer the door.

Clearing his throat, he stood straight and stated, "I would like to talk to Beatrix."

"What's the password?" a black-haired woman asked. She and been at the house weeks before also and had been the one who had given him Beatrix's name the night they had sex in the bathroom, though he didn't know her name, much less a password.

He said the first word he thought of, "Toast."

A brunette popped up and gave him the most surprised expression he had ever seen before. "Holy cow, man, that was it. How did you even know that?"

"Lucky guess," he said, just as a pillow hit him in the head.

"You ass. Get out of the house," Harper stated and came after him at a full run. He may not have played football long, but he knew when he was going to be tackled.

That was until Frankie popped in front of him and took the blonde down with a groan. Instantly, the battle was on, with the brunette hurdling the couch and the black-haired woman rushing his way. Louisa took on the brunette, and he headed for the stairs at a sprint.

It wasn't going to be easy to outrun these women, but he had to try.

Up the stairs, he was happy all the doors were open, and the rooms were empty, except one had a redhead sitting, reading a book on a bed. Dodging hands, he rushed into the room and shut the door, locking it behind him.

Leaning against the door, he could hear someone on the other side trying to open it. First with the nob, then with pounding, and then he was sure with a shoulder. There was a loud thud, then a curse.

"They have the key," Buzz said calmly.

"I don't care. I have you here, and I'll talk to you until they murder me."

"Murder? They wouldn't murder you. Bodies are so hard to hide. But I suggest you pick which limb you can live without before they open the door." She went back to reading, not even caring that he was there.

This is what he had been waiting for: to get her alone and talk to her, though it didn't feel like they were alone with the constant stream of yelling and cursing coming from behind him. But this was his shot, and he was taking it.

"Fine, okay, I came here to tell you that I love you, Beatrix P. Lovely. I want to say I fell for you the moment I saw you, but that was just lust. I think I fell for you when you tackled me. You were willing to put yourself in danger for me and didn't even think of how it would affect you. At the time, I didn't know about your family's fighting skills." He didn't move from the door, in case the constant pounding resulted in it actually opening.

"You can't love me; I'm just like my mother, remember?" She reminded him as she slammed her book shut.

"You are nothing like your mother, and I wish I'd never said you were. You are complete opposites. She only cares about herself, and you care about everyone but yourself. Having me sign that document proves it. You would face me, tell me about the baby, and face my possible anger just to make sure she never for one moment thinks she isn't loved," he said and walked away from the door for a moment, hoping that the lock held until he could convince her. He needed to get closer to her. He couldn't do this across the room.

She shook her head. "Jonas, you aren't in love with me. You're in shock over the baby. I know how you feel. It took me a little to get my head around it, and I was puking every morning as a reminder. And if you don't want them in the room, you have to move the dresser."

At her words, he tried not to smile as he moved the big piece of furniture the three feet to cover the door. It was heavy, and he wondered how Buzz knew that it could be moved, or how many times she had moved it. Then he sat on the bed, far enough away to not spook her, but close enough that he could touch her if he was brave enough.

Her warning had shown him that she was interested in what he was saying and didn't want their conversations to end. That, or she didn't want her sisters to kill him. Either one was a good sign.

Jonas touched her leg with the tips of his fingers, and when she didn't move, he slid an entire hand over the bare skin of her ankle, missing the feel of her skin under his hand. "No, I was in shock in my office. That's how you got away from me before I could tell you that I want you in my life. That you *are* my life."

CHAPTER THIRTY-TWO

"BECAUSE OF THE BABY," she stated the obvious as she ignored his touch. If there weren't a baby, he wouldn't be there.

But the fact that he would say the words, even without meaning them, meant that he was going to love their baby just as much as she already did. It should've made her happy, but it didn't.

She tried to shake his hand loose from her leg, not needing his touch and all the confusion it brought. Her heart sank when he let go.

"Buzz," he said with a smile, shifting on the bed to get closer to her, taking her hand in his. "It's because I love you, baby or not. From the moment I met you, you turned my life upside down and sideways, and I couldn't right myself again. After a while, I didn't want to. My life had been boring before, predictable. I needed you to throw some wildness in for me. I need you in my life."

Sitting up, she looked into his eyes, trying to see if he was lying. Instead of looking into his brown eyes, she just saw the faint purple ring around the left one. "Do you have a black eye?"

Blinking, he touched it and laughed. "Yeah, Louisa popped me for lying to you. She's been taking a boxing class. She's getting pretty good."

"Louisa? Louisa May Alcott Raiden?" Buzz couldn't imagine the girl actually doing it, and the only image that came into her mind made her laugh out loud.

She stopped laughing as he nodded and touched her cheek. A delicate touch, as if he were amazed he could touch her. "Did you know she was named after a children's book author?"

"Of course. We all are," she said hoarsely.

Out in the hallway, voices started yelling about the key being found. The key must have been missing from the secret hook Sera had for them. Lucy had found it years before, and after that, no room was lockable in the house for long.

"We all, as in all your sisters?" He smiled, not turning away from her as the lock turned and the door opened fast, only to slam into the back of the dresser, followed instantly by another loud curse from the hallway.

Ignoring the commotion, she said, "Yes, all of us. Beatrix Potter, and … never mind, I forgot you don't do literature."

When she had been serving one evening for the family, he had told Judith that, something that the woman had dismissed. Buzz had been trying to find clues at the time, and that was a big one.

"I like literature; I just don't talk about it with Judith. Your middle name is really just Potter?" he asked.

Beyond them, a sister issued a series of threats to both of them through the door, with one arm suddenly visible. Harper's voice hissed, "Beatrix Potter Lovely, move that damn dresser so we can beat the crap out of your man."

Rolling her eyes at her sister, Buzz turned to the door and yelled, "Leave us alone, Harper! We are talking. I'll send him out when you've settled down." The movement dislodged his hand, which drifted down to her shoulder.

"Just let me in, me alone. I promise to do nothing to him." Harper's arm was still waving in the air, but her voice was suddenly sugary-sweet as she spoke, as if her past remarks would be forgotten that easily.

"Just leave, all of you." Buzz got off the bed with a huff, tired of her sisters. She slapped at the arm until it left the room, and she shut the door again. This time nobody tried to open it, though she could hear them still talking out in the hallway, planning. Turning to Jonas, she stated, "You, of course, may leave also."

"Except I'll never walk away from you and our baby again." He jumped up and took her hand, leading her back to her bed. Sitting down, he pulled her between his legs, resting his hands on her hips to keep her there. He held her captive, but she could've easily gotten away from him. She didn't, though. She couldn't.

It was the same position she had been in when he'd first gotten a good look at her. That night, she had messed up not only the story she needed but her life as well. Now months later, her life was completely different, and she was never going to be the same Buzz again. That Buzz wasn't madly in love with this man.

"Jonas," she whispered. She had no idea what else to say. She wanted to stay in that spot forever, and she wanted to run away as fast as she could. It was the exact same as she had felt that night, but for all different reasons.

Taking her hands in his, she looked into his eyes as he spoke, "Buzz-Buzz Lovely, can we turn this thing around? We did everything backward. Let's start with me saying I love you and end with you coming out of my closet. Start with us having a baby Buzz, our own baby." He leaned forward and kissed her belly over the pink T-shirt, causing her heart to skip a beat.

She giggled at his words but didn't dare reply. He pulled her closer to him as he slid his hands under her shirt. His fingers skimming over her skin caused her to suck in a breath. "Your shirt says your name on it. And I seem to remember seeing another just like it in white."

She looked down at it and bit her lip. She had way too many of the shirts, but nobody ever took them. "I sleep in them."

"Not when I sleep with you." His hands slid around to her butt and squeezed it.

Ignoring the need to touch him like he was touching her, she shook her head. "Just other times."

"I like them, but I like you even better without them." He pulled her onto his lap, and she went willingly, too willingly.

She snuggled into him and wrapped her arms around him. Buzz breathed in his familiar scent as she reveled being in his arms again, knowing that she was only letting herself believe him because she wanted to so much.

Feeling him kiss her hair, he promised, "I am going to spend the rest of my life loving you and hoping that you can one day love me."

Nuzzling into his neck, she whispered the words that she had known and held close to herself for so long, words she was planning on keeping to herself until the end of time. Except they were bubbling out, and she couldn't stop them.

Pulling back, he looked into her eyes in question. "What did you say?"

"I already love you, Jonas," she said the words again, this time with more conviction. Instantly, he crushed her to him for a kiss, a deep kiss that she returned with the same passion as he was putting into it.

When he pulled away, he touched her cheek. "I have missed you so much. I should have come back for you the day I walked away from here."

"Why didn't you?"

"Fear."

"Of my sisters?" she questioned, wondering what he had gone through to get to her room.

The smile that came to his lips made her heart melt. "No, I'd fight every one of them for you, to see you. I was afraid you didn't feel what I was feeling. That I was just a story for you."

"You stopped being a story before I left that closet, Jonas. At that moment, I wanted you at any cost: My dignity as a reporter. My job as a reporter. My family, because Sera was going to kill me for finding you after she had forbidden it. And I lost everything except my family. That grew because of you, in more ways than one."

"*Our* family from now on." He kissed her cheek. "I know you said you weren't reporting anymore, but if you want to, you can. You can do anything you want to."

"I wasn't very good at it," she admitted, hating to say it.

"I read everything you'd ever written. You just never got the chance to show them how good you were. Maybe another paper will give you that chance. I don't want you to give up your dream because of a story about me turning bad." His hands were inching up her skin under her shirt. It was distracting.

"I don't. Not ever. I don't know what I want to do, but I don't want to go back," she said, leaning into his body. "I don't want to work for Kaine anymore either. I just want to focus on you and our baby for a while."

"Then don't. Do whatever you want. But I do want you to live with me and be a part of my life, to be my life." He kissed her gently.

There was nothing left to do but let him kiss her, and kiss him she did until he took over. Laying her on the bed his magical fingers started working her body over just like they had the first time. Only this time was better because this time, she knew him, loved him, and knew he loved her just as much.

This time there was nothing hiding in the closet.

EPILOGUE

THE WEDDING WAS JUST over twelve hours away as the clock struck midnight. The entire family was staying at the Beckman hotel, all on Cliff as a wedding present to them. Though Sera had tried to get the venue of the wedding changed three times, Buzz had held her ground: no cathedral. Jonas hadn't been to any of the weddings Sera had put on, but he felt he had missed a lot.

Since the girls were spending the evening in their hotel suite, the guys had gone to the bar for a few drinks. Jonas had gotten to know Cliff and Kaine over the last three weeks, and Harrison had forgiven him for what had happened in Jonas's office. So had Sera, but just barely.

It seemed like every man was programmed to leave once the clock struck midnight, even if their wives were locked in a two-bedroom suite that was supposed to hold the five Lovely sisters, Sera, Sera's two girls, and Louisa and Frankie. Those two had been accepted into the fold instantly. Though they still lived in Chicago, they had come back for the wedding.

"One more?" he asked the guys, who were already on their feet.

"Nope, Sera is coming back to sleep with me. We're going to enjoy a night without the girls in the house." Harrison grinned. Jonas wanted to tease him about kids getting in the way of his sex life but thought better of it.

It had only been days after news of Buzz's baby came out that Sera had made her own announcement. She had been holding it back for weeks because she wanted to make the announcement special, except she'd ended up blurting it out when Buzz had told her she and Jonas wanted to get married. It seemed she was overly relieved that she wouldn't look pregnant when one of her kids got married. Then she forbade the last two singles in the house from meeting the man of their dreams until after her baby was born.

Instead, he questioned the man, "I thought the girls were all staying in one room, doing what girls do?"

"They were supposed to, but my Mrs. can't sleep if I'm not around," Cliff stated, draining his beer.

"Harper's going to make everyone stay in that room." Kaine couldn't stop the chuckle that followed. His wife's control over her sisters was only in her head. Everyone knew it, even Jonas knew.

"Am I going to be the only one sleeping alone tonight?" he asked the group as they headed for the door. No one answered.

"Just a heads-up, man. Don't sex up your fiancé too much tonight," Cliff whispered beside him.

Jonas laughed. "I'm assuming she'll stay with her sisters tonight. That's what she said she was going to do—enjoy her time with them since we've been living together for almost three weeks now."

It was all she could talk about for days, even if she spent a lot of time at the Lovely house. They had even slept over twice. But he was beginning to realize there was never too much sister time.

"Just keep your pants on, man. That's my word of advice." Cliff winked at him.

Jonas asked in confusion. "For marriage?"

"Nope, my marriage advice is to always say yes to your Lovely lady, even when it leads you places you don't want to go. You'll want to be there with her."

"That is good advice," Jonas admitted, not thinking anything that profound would come out of the man's mouth since he was usually joking.

"I know. Now I have to go tell my wife yes," Cliff stated with a smile and a salute.

Laughing as the man headed down the hallway towards his room, Jonas wondered if his wife was going to be waiting for him. Buzz had said it was strictly going to be a girl's night, and the men were only invited because Sera wanted everyone in the hotel and ready for the wedding. It seemed there was going to be a lot of sneaking around going on tonight.

When the women had picked a room with two adjoining suites and a total of four beds, he wondered how the seven sisters, their mom, and his two sisters were going to fit. But if those with a spouse were just going to leave, there would be room.

This morning, Sera had cornered him and demanded that he get to bed early, which hadn't happened because Harrison and the guys had wanted to go out for drinks. Sera had been sure that nobody would get enough sleep tonight at the hotel, which was why she was against the idea. It seemed that during every other wedding, everyone had been over-tired on the wedding day. She couldn't figure out why.

After slipping into his own room, he kicked off his shoes, hating not spending the night with Buzz. He was so used to her being there beside him that he was dreading that night and hoped that there wouldn't be another like it in a long time.

Though it was the same hotel, it wasn't the room he'd had months before when he had met Buzz the first time. But it was a carbon copy, which only made him miss her more.

Then it hit him. If the wives weren't staying in the girl's room, was it possible that Buzz was going to come to his room? That it had been the plan the entire time? Instantly, he pulled off his T-shirt and tossed it on the floor on the way to the bedroom.

Except he didn't think she was there. Last time he had sensed she was there, and this time, nothing. If she were there, he would know it. Now that he loved her, he should know when she is in a room.

Which left him nothing else to do but go to bed and hope that morning came quickly.

Not half an hour later, there was a knock on the door, a quiet one that left him wondering if he had heard it at all. Sitting up and shaking himself from sleep, he smiled. There she was—his sneaky little soon-to-be wife.

Walking to the door in just his boxers, he didn't even check to make sure it was her before swinging the door open to invite her in.

But instead of his redhead, it was four of her sisters, two of whom where his also. They all looked from his face and down his body, then at the ceiling quickly.

"Nice way to greet family, Jonas," Frankie stated flatly.

"Get some pants on, man. Nobody wants to see that. Least of all us," Agatha added.

Turning away as he pulled his pants on, he wondered exactly why they were there. Was Buzz getting cold feet? This afternoon, she had been upset that their wedding was taking too long to actually happen. Could she have changed her mind after all?

"Where is Buzz?" he asked the moment he was out in the living room area of the suite. All four sisters were sitting and looking at their respective phones.

"Here," Lucy stated as she put her phone away.

Every one of the women were in their pajamas, and not a one looked like they had been sleeping, which meant they would be tired the next day, and Sera would be mad.

"I haven't seen her," he said when there was another knock on the door.

But when he opened it, it was only Cliff carrying Mabel, and she was trying not to giggle.

"Put me down. You win!" He dipped her head towards the floor, and she squealed a little before saying again, "You win!"

"Gross, you two. Aren't you married now? Stop it," Lucy said, but she was smiling as she watched Cliff set his wife on her feet and give her a kiss on the lips.

"Let's start this thing," Agatha stated from the couch.

Cliff looked over at her. "Not everyone is here, Ag."

"Enough are. We can't keep doing this with everyone. There gets to be too many," Agatha grumbled as another knock came on the door.

Jonas went and opened it for Harper and Kaine, who hurried in like they were being followed. They were also in pajamas, and Jonas realized that all the women were wearing "Buzzzz" T-shirts in assorted colors.

"Nice that you're dressed, Jonas. Is Buzz?" Cliff grinned at him, his wife still in his arms.

"Buzz isn't here," he replied, now starting to worry where she was. Everyone was here, and they all seemed to think she should be here also.

"Where's Buzz? Who saw her last?"

"She left our room before Sera did, which was almost two hours ago," Louisa stated, looking at her phone, then looked up. "Where is she? Was she kidnapped or something?"

"I thought this was a nice hotel, Cliff. Not one a woman could get kidnapped from." Mabel slapped him on the arms as she said it.

"Who would kidnap her? I mean, the red hair is kind of cool, but not hold-for-days cool," Harper said and wedged herself on the couch between Agatha and Frankie, taking Frankie's phone from her and looking at it. The blue-haired woman quickly took it back.

"Where was she going when she left?" Kaine asked, leaning against the door. There was very little space in the room.

"Here. She even had a keycard," Louisa answered. Jonas could tell she was getting panicky, which, in turn, was making him nervous.

"Okay, we split up and search the room. Kaine and Harper, you are team one. Maby and Cliff, team two. Agatha, you take Frankie, me, and Louisa." Lucy jumped from the couch and started paring everyone off.

"Why so many teams, and why is Jonas with no one?" Harper demanded, pointing at him. Her purple shirt had "Buzz" in neon yellow letters.

"I want Louisa. She's really good at hide and seek," Frankie stated at the same time.

"Stop!" Jonas yelled, bringing everyone's attention to him. "No teams. I don't think the room is that big."

He left them and went into the bedroom, which he knew she wasn't in. He had just been there himself, and she wasn't there. But it had to be searched before everyone walked into the room.

It took less than a minute to find her sleeping on the floor in the closet. Opening the closed door, he saw her in the same spot she had been in months before. Only this time, she was curled into a ball, silently sleeping.

Crouching down, he touched her shoulder. "Buzz, wake up."

She jerked and opened her eyes. He could tell she was still mostly asleep when she smiled at him and then rolled into a tighter ball. Instantly, he wrapped his arms around her and lifted her from the closet.

"Jonas?" her voice was thick with sleep as her arms went around him.

Kissing the top of her head as she rested it against his chest, he asked, "What are you doing in the closet?"

"Waiting for you to come back from the bar. I was going to come out of the closet and sex you up, but I fell asleep." She opened her eyes and scowled at the room as if it were the room's fault.

All he could do was laugh at her cute little scowl. He wished he had found her when he had gotten back from the bar, but the door had been closed, and he didn't even think to look in there. That was never going to happen again.

"You'll have to sex me up later," he whispered, noticing Cliff and Mabel in the doorway.

"No, I can do it now." She squirmed in his arms, not noticing they had company. "Just give me a moment."

"Wedding time, Buzz," Cliff stated from where he stood.

Jonas gathered her closer to him. There was only one thing she needed now, despite her words: to go back to sleep. "That's tomorrow, Cliff. Now Buzz needs to get some sleep."

Buzz instantly smiled and giggled. "No, Jonas, we have to get married."

"Tomorrow, honey." He kissed her again. She wasn't fully awake yet. Hopefully, she would fall back to sleep quickly. Then he could get rid of her family.

"No, Honey," Cliff mocked his nickname for his soon-to-be wife. "The judge is here, and he doesn't like to linger."

"Cliff is right. We have to get married now. It's tradition." Buzz wiggled until he put her down.

"We're getting married in a few hours, Buzz," he reminded her, wondering how long she thought she had slept.

Buzz went back into the closet and reappeared in tight gray jogging pants. "No, we are getting married now, just like all my sisters. It's tradition."

"Lovely's marry before the big Sera wedding. So far, everyone else has," Mabel filled him in.

"Let's get it over with," Buzz said and headed out of the bedroom.

Once they were back in the living room, he saw the new arrival, who was not happy to be there. Within minutes they were married, or so the paper said. Harper had insisted she be a witness, and nobody could talk her down. Louisa was the other signer because Frankie refused.

Once the document was signed, everyone was gone from the room in two minutes, everyone but Buzz and him and a piece of paper that said she was his.

"What was that?" Jonas asked when the door closed behind the last wedding guest. He supposed that was what they were called.

Buzz grabbed the paper from the table and looked at it for a moment before putting it down again. "That was a Lovely wedding. Sera never lets anyone just get married in a simple ceremony, so we do it the night before. Cliff has something over the judge. You can't tell Sera about this, or she'll be pissed."

"You mean we have to go ahead with the other wedding?" he asked. It seemed like a weird and unnecessary tradition.

Buzz spun and looked at him as if he just wasn't smart enough to catch on. "Of course. That one is for Sera. Cliff and Maby started it, and it has been my favorite part of all the weddings."

"Is that why you went with almost everything Sera wanted? Except for the venue?" She'd seemed okay with so much, he thought that she wanted it all. There were even fireworks!

Buzz shrugged. "I put up a fight on enough so that she didn't get suspicious."

"You weren't going to tell me about it?" There hadn't been a single hint about it. Not once. Though the wedding planning had been fast, he thought she could have found time to tell him about the pre-wedding wedding.

"I was going to tonight, but I fell asleep before I could seduce you." She grinned. She was lying. They hadn't been together long, but he knew her good enough to know when she was lying to him. This was all going to be a surprise wedding for him. Or a pre-wedding wedding.

With a shake of the head, he let it go. He was getting used to her surprising him. So far, a few of the surprises hadn't been nice ones. Walking over to her, he pulled her into his arms. "Can you seduce me now?"

She shrugged and looked up at him. "Now? I don't know, I'm kind of tired, and I already have you locked down."

Dropping a kiss by her ear, he whispered, "What if I came out of the closet?"

She threw her head back in a laugh. "I can work with that."

Lifting her into his arms, he carried her into the bedroom. Neither went into the closet or came out of it, though they argued about it before neither could talk anymore. And neither wanted to.

The End

Thank you so much for reading Falling for his Step-Sister.

The next Lovely to fall in love is Lucy Maude in Falling for his Fake Wife.

ABOUT ALIE GARNETT

I love to read and prefer a little spice in those books. I am lucky enough to live on a small hobby farm in northern Minnesota with her husband and two kids. I enjoy spending time in the pasture with my two mini horses and one fainting goat (who doesn't actually faint). When I'm not writing, I'm busy trying to do all the things I didn't get to while writing. Or maybe I wouldn't have gotten to them anyway, because its laundry, dishes and fun things like that.

ALSO BY ALIE GARNETT

<u>Indulge</u>

Craving Winter

Enticing Aurora

<u>Landstad, ND</u>

Invisible

Irresistible

Impulsive

Insuppressible

Intriguing

Imperfect

Irreplaceable

<u>The Great Lovely Falls</u>

Falling for the Single Mom

Falling for his Best Friends Sister

Falling for the Boss

Falling for his Step-Sister

Falling for his Fake Wife

Falling into a Second Chance

<u>Hart Series</u>

Seeing her Pain

Her Favor

Max Valentine is Looking at Me!

Keeping her Safe

<u>Stand Alone</u>
Romancing the Doctor